"This is all about busi...

Sabrina licked her bottom lip and Billy had the urge to lean down and catch the plump flesh between his teeth and nibble. "My business. FindMeACowboy.com."

"Sounds highly illegal."

A grin tugged at her full lips. "It's a dating service."

"Why cowboys?"

"Because they're generally hard workers, trustworthy, loyal." She arched an eyebrow at him. "Have you ever thought about meeting someone online?"

"I meet plenty of women as it is, and I barely have time for any of them. I ride bulls for a living, and I'm this close to my first championship."

"Yet here you are dancing with me." Despite the stiff way she held herself, there was just something about the way she looked at him with those deep blue eyes that said she was hungry for more than she wanted to admit. "One would be inclined to think you're looking for someone."

"Maybe, but this isn't about a date."

"What is it about?"

"It's about sex, darlin'." Billy pulled her closer, plastering them together from chest to thigh, holding her securely with one arm around her waist.

"Lots of breath-stealing, bone-melting *sex...*"

Dear Reader,

For those of you who read my January Harlequin Blaze
book, *Texas Outlaws: Jesse,* you'll recognize bad-boy
pro bull rider Billy Chisholm. He's back, and he's hot on
the trail of city girl Sabrina Collins. Billy and Sabrina are
interested in only one thing—sex. Sabrina is busy launching
her website, FindMeACowboy.com, and the last thing she
has time for is an actual relationship. And with a cowboy?
No, thank you. While Sabrina might see the appeal of the
rugged, Wrangler-wearing types, she certainly doesn't want
a relationship with one for herself. A few hours of breath-
stealing, mind-blowing sex is about all she can fit into her
schedule.

Ditto for Billy. He's this close to landing the first of a series
of wins that will take him straight to the PBR finals. But he
needs a distraction, and what better way to take the edge
off than a little roll in the hay?

I hope you enjoy watching Sabrina and Billy fall madly,
desperately in lust, and love! Life is real and so is the
connection, both physical and emotional, that brings a man
and woman together. The Blaze line gives me the freedom
to portray both and I'm so happy to be back this month
with the second installment in my new trilogy featuring the
sexy Chisholm brothers.

Much love from deep in the heart,

Kimberly Raye

P.S. Don't forget to stop by and visit me on the web at
www.kimberlyraye.com or friend me on Facebook. I love
hearing from readers!

Texas Outlaws: Billy

—

Kimberly Raye

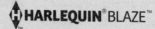
HARLEQUIN® BLAZE™

ISBN-13: 978-0-373-79788-2

TEXAS OUTLAWS: BILLY

Copyright © 2014 by Kimberly Groff

Printed in U.S.A.

HARLEQUIN®
www.Harlequin.com

ABOUT THE AUTHOR

USA TODAY bestselling author Kimberly Raye started her first novel in high school and has been writing ever since. To date, she's published more than fifty novels, two of them prestigious RITA® Award nominees. She's also been nominated by *RT Book Reviews* for several Reviewer's Choice Awards, as well as a career achievement award. Currently she is writing a romantic vampire mystery series for Ballantine Books that is in development with ABC for a television pilot. She also writes steamy contemporary reads for Harlequin's Blaze line. Kim lives deep in the heart of the Texas Hill Country with her very own cowboy, Curt, and their young children. She's an avid reader who loves Diet Dr. Pepper, chocolate, Toby Keith, chocolate, alpha males (*especially* vampires) and chocolate. Kim also loves to hear from readers. You can visit her online at www.kimberlyraye.com.

Books by Kimberly Raye

HARLEQUIN BLAZE

*The Texas Outlaws

This book is for Josh.

You've turned into a fine young man
and I couldn't be more proud of you!

Go Tarleton Texans!

1

PRO BULL RIDER William Bonney Chisholm had a hard-on the size of Texas.

He stood smack-dab in the middle of the kick-off dance for the Lost Gun Fair and Rodeo, a three-week-long event taking place at the fairgrounds on the outskirts of town. The band had started up. Couples two-stepped across the dance floor. The pungent scent of beer and livestock teased his nostrils. Cigarette smoke cluttered the air.

Easy, bud. Easy.

He shifted and damned himself for being such a sucker for the opposite sex. Blondes, in particular.

He'd fallen hard and fast years back the first moment he'd set eyes on Tami Elder's Malibu Barbie. Tami had taken riding lessons at the ranch where Billy and his two older brothers had grown up. They'd been taken in by rodeo star Pete Gunner after their crook of a father had died in a house fire. Since Billy's mother had passed years before that and the Gunner spread was an all-male domain—home to the infamous Lost Boys, a cracker-jack group of young riders trained and honed by pro bull rider Pete Gunner himself—the only female Billy had ever kept company with had been a paint horse by the name of Lula Bell.

Until Tami had started coming out to the ranch every Sunday. He'd done his best, like any ten-year-old boy when faced with a cootie-carrying girl, to make her life a living hell. He'd shot spit wads while she'd rubbed down her horse and fired his water gun at her while she'd trotted around the corral.

He'd hated her, and she'd hated him, and all had been right with his male-dominated world. Then one hot summer afternoon, everything had changed. That had been the summer he'd turned eleven and spied his oldest brother, Jesse, kissing Susie Alexander, the local rodeo queen.

Kissing, of all things.

Billy had been hurt, then he'd been mad, and then he'd glimpsed an actual tongue and he'd been damned interested. For a little while. Then he'd been mad again and he'd raced off to gather some chinaberries for his slingshot. To see how many shots it took to get his brother away from Miss Travis County.

He'd been up in a nearby tree counting his berries when Tami had finished her riding lesson. She'd slid off the horse and wandered over to the tree, her doll case in hand, to play until her dad finished talking to the riding instructor. He'd meant to shoot off a few practice shots at her, but then her dad had called her over. He'd climbed down and had been about to stomp the day-lights out of her Barbie when he'd realized that it wasn't just any old Barbie.

It was a naked one.

Just like that, his belief system had done a complete one-eighty. One glance at all those interesting curves and that long blond hair and those deep blue eyes, and he'd started to wonder at the possibilities when it came to the real thing.

Yep, he loved blondes.

The trouble was, the pretty little thing standing near the bar was a brunette.

His gaze swept from her long, wavy brown hair pulled back in a loose ponytail to the shiny tips of her black stilettos, and back up again. She looked nothing like the other buckle bunnies crowding the dance floor. No itty-bitty tank tops or scandalous Daisy Duke shorts. Instead, she wore a black skirt that accented her tiny waist and a sleeveless black blouse that fell softly against a modest pair of breasts. There was nothing voluptuous about her. Nothing outright sexy.

Ah, but there was something about the way she stood there, her back so stiff and straight, her lips parted slightly as she sipped from a red plastic cup, that made his adrenaline pump that much faster.

She was a yuppie through and through. Out of her element, given the three-inch heels and what he would be willing to bet was wine in her glass. Probably a big-city reporter who'd gotten stuck covering the local rodeo.

He would have figured her for one of the big-time

reporters who'd been in attendance to cover the "Where Are They Now?" episode of *Famous Texas Outlaws,* a documentary that had featured his father and the crime that had brought a wave of notoriety crashing down on the small town of Lost Gun, Texas. The original episode had aired just six years after his father's death, and the "Where Are They Now?" follow-up just two short weeks ago.

But most of the press had all cleared out, making way for the influx of rodeo riders and fans who'd come from all over the state for the best little rodeo in Texas.

Still, she had that big-city look about her.

She didn't belong here, and damned if that didn't pique his curiosity. A man could only drink black coffee so many mornings before he started hankering for something different. Maybe a few packets of sugar to sweeten things up. Or one of those fancy lattes with all the whipped cream.

A vision hit him, of her naked beneath him, whipped cream covering the really interesting parts, and his groin throbbed. He shifted, eager to give himself a few precious inches of breathing room. No such luck. He'd been training for weeks, straddling the celibacy horse in order to maintain his focus. Tomorrow was his chance. His first shot at riding his way straight into the champion's seat. His brother Jesse, the current PBR champ, had just announced his intention to marry the love of his life and start a business breeding his own bucking bulls. After sweeping the preliminaries with perfect scores just a few days before, he'd decided to pull out of the local rodeo. He was ready to step down from professional bull riding completely and turn his attention to something more long-term. Which meant every bull rider from here to kingdom come was gunning for that top spot.

But the winner's seat belonged to Billy.

He'd waited too long for this shot, worked too hard. He wasn't letting anything mess it up and he wasn't letting anyone beat him.

All the more reason to turn and get while the getting was good. Billy had come out tonight to have a few beers and relax. To lose the nerves.

He'd had a shitty training session today and all because he was wound tighter than a rattlesnake about to strike. He'd gone four days without a decent night's sleep. Four days of tossing and turning and visualizing the semifinals coming up in eight days. He needed a good strong ride to push him into the finals. And he needed *great* to actually win.

And he had to win.

Because even more than the title, Billy had several sponsorships riding on this next win. Big money all looking to back the next superstar since they were losing Jesse. And if there was one thing Billy liked, it was money. Before Pete had taken him in, Billy and his brothers had grown up dirt-poor without a pot to piss in. Their dad had spent his time drinking himself into a stupor and looking for the next big score instead of taking care of his three boys. That had meant cheese sandwiches for dinner every night.

When they'd had dinner, that is.

There'd been too many times when they'd had nothing at all. No food on the table. No shoes on their feet. No decent clothes on their backs. No bed to lay their heads. He and his brothers had spent more than one night in the backseat of their dad's broken-down Chevy because the old man had gone on a drinking binge, thanks to some moneymaking heist gone wrong.

Billy had been young at the time, only eight when Silas Chisholm had died in that fire after the biggest score of his life had earned him two minutes of fame and a feature spot in the hour-long *Famous Texas Outlaws*.

More like *Stupid Texas Outlaws*. The old man had been celebrating with a case of white lightning that had made him more than a little careless with a lit cigarette. He'd set himself on fire and taken the money with him.

At least that's what everyone thought.

Billy ignored the mess of questions swimming in his head. Questions that had just started to surface, thanks to a surge of new interest sparked by the anniversary of the documentary and his oldest brother's crazy intuition.

Jesse had dropped the bomb just a few days ago that he felt certain the money was still out there and that Silas had had a partner in the heist. His older brother had even uncovered said partner's identity.

Not that Billy gave a shit about any of it. He was more content to let sleeping dogs lie. To stop trying to dig up the past and just leave it six feet under where it belonged.

He wanted to forget those early days. The cold upholstery beneath his cheek. The hunger eating at his gut.

The uncertainty knocking in his chest. And the bitter fact that out of all three boys, Billy was a chip off the old block. The spitting image of his father.

The same hair.

The same eyes.

The same, period.

Like *hell*.

He might look like the old man, but he wasn't following the same miserable path. He was going to ride his ass off, impress as many sponsors as possible and bring home a win.

Hopefully.

He stiffened against the niggling doubt and took another drink of his beer.

He needed to get out of his head and breathe for a little while. Maybe talk shop with the other contestants and see who posed the biggest threat. He had an idea, since he'd been following all of his fellow contenders, but still. It was good to see them face-to-face, to look deep into their eyes and see the drive. The determination. To see who messed up tonight by drinking too much, or staying out too late, or carousing with too many women. All three were distractions better avoided.

Which was why Billy sure as shootin' wasn't out tonight looking to get laid. No matter how much he suddenly wanted to.

Hell, no.

He tugged at the top button of his shirt and tossed down another swallow of Coors Light. Neither did much to cool the fiery lust burning him up from the inside out. Tossing down another long swallow, he turned his attention to the old cowboy standing next to him.

Eli McGinnis was the grandfather that Billy had never had. He looked as if he'd stepped straight out of a Larry McMurtry novel with his snow-white slicked back hair and a handlebar mustache that curled up at the ends. He wore a plaid Western shirt starched within an inch of its life, a pair of Wranglers and a knowing expression that said he'd been there and done that a dozen times over. An old rodeo cowboy, he'd been a permanent fixture at the Gunner spread for as long as Billy could remember. A mentor to all of the Lost Boys, Billy included. Eli had also been instrumental in Billy's success on the rodeo circuit. The old cowboy had been handing out advice and badgering him into hanging on just a little longer, a little tighter, a little *more,* for years now.

"…make sure your hand's under the rope real solid before you even think about giving the signal."

"Got it."

"And keep your back bowed, but not too bowed."

"Will do."

"And get your eyeballs back into your head."

"Already done—" The comment cut off as Billy's head snapped up. He stared into the old man's knowing gaze. "What the hell are you talking about, Eli?"

"That uppity-up over yonder." Eli motioned across the sawdust floor. "If you keep staring at her like that, she's liable to burst into flames right here and now."

"You're losin' it, old man. I'm doing no such thing. My mind's all about tomorrow."

"True enough, but to get to tomorrow, you've got to make it through tonight."

"What are you trying to say?"

"Landsakes, do I have to spell it out for you?" He gave Billy a nudge. "Get your ass over there and dance with the woman. Otherwise, you'll keep wonderin' and that sure as shit's gonna kill your concentration and lead to another sleepless night. Better to blow off some steam and get your mind off everything for a little while."

"I thought it was better to avoid any and all distractions."

"Yeah, but if that isn't working out too well, you have to move on to plan B."

"Which is?"

"Just get to it and get it out of your system."

Billy glanced across the dance floor, his gaze colliding with the hot brunette's. The air rushed from his lungs in that next instant, and for a split second he forgot to breathe.

A crazy reaction. But then that's what happened when a twenty-six-year-old, red-blooded male in his prime went without sex for four months and six days and two hours and twenty-nine minutes.

Lust.

That's all it was.

And nerves.

Tomorrow was big. The first official day of training for the semifinal round that would, hopefully, lead him straight to the finals. The press would be there. The rodeo officials. The fans. All watching and speculating.

It made sense he'd be a little nervous. Not scared, mind you. More like anxious. Excited.

He sure as hell wasn't getting all worked up because of the way her eyes sparkled and her lips curved into a smile.

A *smile,* for Christ's sake.

"Maybe you're right," he heard himself say. "Maybe I should just get to it."

"The sooner you start, the sooner it ends." Eli nodded. "Then you can get focused again and forget all about those long legs and that tiny little waist and those really big—"

"Enough," he cut in. "I get the point."

"Then stop talking and start walking."

"Yes, boss." He left the old man grinning after him and headed across the dance floor.

2

SABRINA COLLINS NEEDED a cowboy in the *worst* way.

One hundred and fifty of them to be exact, which was the *only* reason she'd agreed to leave her L.A. apartment and head for a place like Lost Gun, Texas.

The small town played host to one of the biggest rodeos in the state, which had started a few days ago with several preliminary events. The official start, however, was tonight's dance. While the town was little more than a map dot, for the next few weeks it would be *the* place to be for rodeo fans across the nation. Particularly the male variety.

On top of that, the town had gained recent notoriety thanks to a documentary featuring famous Texas outlaws. Lost Gun had started out over one hundred and fifty years ago as a haven for outlaws and criminals, and so it had been a natural pick for the documentary crew who'd not only played up the town's history but also focused on a crime committed by one of Lost Gun's very own who'd robbed a local bank and then bit the bullet in a house fire. The money had supposedly perished in the fire, but the television host had raised enough questions to make viewers think that the treasure might still be out there. The town had been a go-to spot for fortune seekers ever since.

Not that Sabrina was interested in a bunch of treasure hunters.

She wanted cowboys. Hot, handsome, *real* cowboys.

Just like the one headed straight for her.

He had short blond hair and chiseled features. The faintest shadow of a beard covered his strong jaw. A white cotton T-shirt—the words *Cowboy Tuff* blazing in red letters across the front—framed his massive shoulders and hugged his thick biceps. Worn, faded denim cupped his crotch and molded to trim hips and long, muscular legs. His scuffed brown boots had obviously seen better days, but then that was the way every cowboy worth his salt liked them.

She could still remember the boys back in her small-town high school, a map dot in East Texas that wasn't so different from this one. The boys back home would rather duct-tape their favorite boots than give them up for a shiny new pair.

There was no duct tape in sight, but this guy still looked every bit as wild as any wrangler she'd left behind when she'd rolled out of Sugar Creek and headed for UCLA.

Sabrina's fingers tightened around the plastic cup in her hand and a shiver of excitement worked its way up her spine.

Because he was a cowboy and another name to add to her currently growing database.

She certainly wasn't feeling all tingly because of the way he looked at her. As if he wanted to take several slow bites and savor each one.

No biting.

No savoring.

No.

She pulled a business card from her purse that listed her email address and her cell phone number.

Numbers. It was all about the numbers.

That's what Mitch, team leader for the investment firm, had told her when she'd approached them about fronting the start-up cash for a new online-dating service that specialized in Western singles. The service was the brainchild of Sabrina and her two college roommates, Livi Hudson and Katherine Ramsey. Since Sabrina knew how to write, she'd penned the business model, while Livi focused on the marketing and Kat handled the actual web design. The idea had grown out of yet another bad breakup for Livi, followed by a night of apple martinis and *Bonanza* reruns.

Forget the bank executives and the grungy tattoo artists and the egocentric personal trainers. Livi wanted a real man. A man's man.

A cowboy.

And if she wanted one, then there had to be a ton of other women out there who did, too, right?

Sabrina hadn't been as convinced, but money talks and polls on Facebook and Twitter had convinced her that Livi's idea might be just the ticket to becoming her own boss.

The three had set up a website, done some soft-launch testing at various singles events and now it was time to put up or shut up. If they could prove to potential investors that they could stock their database with an adequate number of profiles, both men and women, then Southern Money International would front the initial capital needed to officially launch FindMeACowboy.com. They'd given the trio three months to build their singles database.

That had been two months and two weeks ago and while Sabrina and her besties had managed to sign up a decent number of females, they were falling a little short when it came to eligible males.

Men were crucial.

Tall, strong, Stetson-wearing men.

With time running out, Sabrina had had no choice. Kat had stayed back in L.A. to fine-tune the website and finish entering profiles while Sabrina and Livi had headed to Texas. It was Lost Gun or failure.

"Listen, I know this isn't your favorite place, but how bad can it be?"

Sabrina cast a sideways glance at the petite redhead standing next to her at the bar.

Livi shrugged. "Okay, so we're talking bad with a capital *B*. You hate small towns and we're in a small town. Still—" she cast a glance around "—it's kind of fun. I always wanted to learn to two-step."

"And I want to be the next Woodward and Burns."

Or at least, she had back when she'd been a freshman

taking her first journalism class and the real world had been four years away. But entry-level journalist positions were hard to come by, and if she did manage to land one, she wouldn't make enough to cover her rent, much less pay back the mountain of student loans.

Which is the reason that she'd taken a slight vacation from hard-core journalism to write fluff pieces for a few local tabloids and work on FindMeACowboy.com. The fluff coupled with the dating service would pay the bills and then some. Meanwhile, she would keep writing for the few blogs that actually liked her work and build her résumé. She was already brainstorming a new piece— an in-depth look at the bank robbery that had put Lost Gun on the map. Who knew? Maybe she could find a new twist regarding the missing money. She was here, after all. She might as well ask around.

In the meantime, she was going to sign up as many cowboys as possible and get the hell back to the city just as soon as she filled up her database.

"I feel like dancing." Livi's voice pulled her from her thoughts. "I'm going to head over to that table and ask one of those hunks to dance." She indicated a handful of good-looking men in starched Western shirts. "And then I'm going to sign him up and find him the love of his life."

Sabrina smiled as Livi made a beeline for the group. The expression died a heartbeat later when she heard the deep, seductive voice.

"What's the fun in that?"

"Excuse me?" She cast a sideways glance at the hunky cowboy she'd spotted earlier.

Up close he was even more mouthwatering.

"Love." His eyes glittered a hot, potent violet. His lips curved in a sexy smile. "Life isn't about love. It's about lust."

"Is that so?"

He shrugged. "Lust makes the world go 'round."

"So sayeth a commitment-fearing man."

"I don't fear commitment, sugar." He shrugged. "I just don't see the point in it."

"And you are?"

"William Bonney Chisholm—" he touched a tanned finger to the brim of his Stetson and tipped it toward her "—but folks around here just call me Billy."

"As in *the* Billy Chisholm?" Her mind scrambled, recalling bits and pieces from the posters plastered around town and the commentaries airing on the local radio stations. "The bull rider?"

A grin spread from ear to ear. "You've heard about me."

"Actually, I've heard about your brother. He's the current pro bull-riding champion, right?"

"For now. But he's getting slow and preoccupied and I can guaran-damn-tee that another win isn't in the cards for him."

"How can you be so sure?"

"Because he sold out in the name of love and now his concentration's for shit. The only plus is that he smartened up and ran for the hills before he embarrassed himself." He arched an eyebrow. "What's your name?"

"Sabrina Collins."

"You a reporter?" he asked, which made sense since the place was crawling with them.

"I wish." The words were out before she could stop them. She stiffened. "What I mean is, I do have a journalism degree, but I'm not here for that." She handed him her business card. "I'm with FindMeACowboy.com. We're an online-dating service for cowboys and cowgirls, and anyone wanting to meet either one. You'd be perfect for our website."

"What about a dance? Would I work for that?"

Her gaze went to the crowded dance floor filled with sliding boots and swaying Wranglers. "I've never really danced to country music."

He winked. "There's a first time for everything." He touched her and her heart stalled.

And then his strong fingers closed around hers and he led her out to the dance floor.

3

BILLY HAD RUBBED bellies with more than his fair share of women over the years. But none had ever felt as soft or as warm as Sabrina Collins.

The notion struck him the moment he pulled her close and felt her pressed up against his body. He trailed his fingertips down the side of her face, under the curve of her jaw, down the smooth column of her throat, until the silky fabric of her blouse stopped him.

"You don't look like much of a rodeo fan," he murmured.

She shrugged. "Rodeos I can do without. Cowboys are a different matter altogether. I need as many as possible."

"I've heard a lot of pickup lines, but that's a first."

"Don't flatter yourself." She licked her bottom lip and he had the urge to lean down and catch the plump flesh between his teeth and nibble. "This is all about business. My business. FindMeACowboy.com."

"Sounds highly illegal."

A grin tugged at her full lips. "It's a dating service."

"Why cowboys?"

"Because they're generally hard workers, trustworthy, loyal."

"You don't sound one hundred percent convinced." There was a cautious air about her and she seemed to stiffen as he stared down at her.

"It doesn't matter what I believe." She shrugged. "It's about the three thousand, four hundred and seventy-two women that we polled last year. So?" She arched an eyebrow at him. "Have you ever thought about meeting someone online?"

"No."

"Why not?"

"Because I meet plenty of women as it is, and I barely have time for any of them. I ride bulls for a living and this is my year. This rodeo is the first step to my very own championship in the fall. I don't have time for dating."

"Yet here you are dancing with me." Despite the stiff way she held herself, there was just something about the way she looked at him with those deep blue eyes that said she was hungry for more than she wanted to admit. "One would be inclined to think you're looking for someone."

"Maybe, but this isn't about a date."

"What is it about?"

"It's about sex, darlin'." He pulled her closer, plastering them together from chest to thigh, holding her securely with one arm around her waist. "Lots of breath-stealing, bone-melting *sex.*"

Billy's words slid into her ears, coaxing her to soften in his arms the way the warm heat of his body urged her to relax and let her guard down.

Fat chance.

The last thing she needed was to wind up in bed with a cowboy. For all her determination to find as many hunky, Wrangler-wearing hotties as possible, she wasn't looking for one for herself. Sabrina Collins didn't do cowboys. She'd seen firsthand just how unreliable they could be, and she certainly wasn't interested in spending the rest of her life with one.

Then again, Billy Chisholm wasn't exactly proposing marriage.

"You smell like cotton candy," he murmured, his rich, deep voice sizzling over her nerve endings.

"A cotton-candy martini. The out-of-towner special over at the bar. About the sex thing, I'm really not interested."

"Why?"

"I beg your pardon?"

"Don't you like sex?"

She gave him a pointed stare. "Maybe I don't like you."

"Sugar, you don't even know me. I'm a great guy. Awesome." The teasing light in his eyes eased the stiffness in her muscles and she felt the flutter of butterfly wings in her stomach. A good sign if she'd just run into a nice-looking guy at her local Starbucks. But Billy Chis-

holm wasn't your average Joe and she wasn't letting herself get sucked in by his Southern charm.

Still. He talked a good talk. She arched an eyebrow.
"Awesome, huh?"

"In bed and out."

"Most men who walk around talking about how awesome they are in the sack usually aren't much to talk
about."

"I guess you'll just have to find out for yourself."

She wanted to.

Her hands crept up the hard wall of his chest, her
arms twined around his neck and she leaned closer.

His heart beat against her breasts. His warm breath
sent shivers down the bare column of her neck. His
hands splayed at the base of her spine, one urging her
even closer while the other crept its way up, as if memorizing every bump and groove, until he reached her
neck. A few deft movements of his fingers and the tight
ponytail she wore unraveled. Her hair spilled down her
back.

His hand cradled the base of her scalp, massaging for
a few blissful moments, making her legs tremble and
her good intentions scramble.

For the next few moments, she forgot all about her
website and the all-important fact that she was supposed
to be working right now.

She tilted her head back and found him staring down
at her, as if he wanted to scoop her over his shoulder
and haul her home to bed.

She had a quick vision of him wearing nothing but his

cowboy hat, looming over her, his muscles gleaming in the moonlight as he loved her within an inch of her life.

And then walked away the next morning.

And that was the problem in a nutshell.

Sabrina had been there and done that. After she'd left home at eighteen, she'd been hellbent on not falling in love, and so she'd focused on lust. She'd indulged in too many one-night stands during those slutty college years, and beyond. Until she'd watched one of her roommates, Kat, meet the man of her dreams and fall in love. That had been two years ago when Kat had been a kindred spirit. A faithful believer in one-night stands just like Sabrina. Until she'd met Harry. He was an accountant by trade and living proof that there were a few good men out there. He didn't lie or cheat or try to charm his way out of a difficult situation. He relied on honesty and integrity and he made Kat feel like a queen.

Sabrina wanted a Harry of her own and so she'd stopped wasting her time with one-night stands.

Sure, she liked sex, and she sure missed it after eleven months of celibacy—the amount of time since her last relationship—but she also liked camaraderie. She wanted a man to make her pancakes the next morning. A man who called if he was running late after work. A man who wouldn't turn tail and run at the first sign of commitment.

A man who could give her more than just a really great orgasm.

Not that she minded a really great orgasm. But she preferred the friendship that came with an actual relationship. And when she wasn't in a relationship like now? She had a vibrator that could deliver without all the awkwardness that followed a brief sexual encounter.

No fumbling for clothing or making promises that would never be kept. A vibrator was simple. Easy. Honest.

"I really don't think this is a good idea. If you'll excuse me…" She didn't wait for a response. She darted away from him and left him staring after her.

His gaze drilled into her, and it was all she could do to keep from running back and begging him to give her the ride of her life.

He could. She knew it. She felt it.

She headed for the rear exit. Out in the parking lot, she climbed behind the wheel of her ancient Bonneville. She gave one last look at the exit door, half expecting, half hoping that he would come after her. He didn't, and a swell of disappointment went through her, quickly followed by a wave of relief.

The last thing, the very *last* thing she needed in her life, was to fall into bed with the exact type of man she'd sworn off of years ago.

Her father had been a cowboy. A charming, salt-of-the-earth type, who worked from sunrise to sunset and never complained. But while he had a strong work ethic, his moral code had desperately lacked. He'd had an easy grin and a weakness for loose-looking women. He'd cheated on Arlene Collins regularly, always smooth-talking his way back into the house after a night of carousing with every female in their desperately small town. Arlene had forgiven him, catered to him, loved him, in spite of his good-for-nothing ways. She'd been a minister's daughter who'd taken her vows very seriously. Therefore, she'd stuck by him through all the bad times, eager to keep her marriage together and make it work. But she'd never really been happy because Dan Collins hadn't been a forever kind of man. He'd been the play-the-field, charm-you-out-of-your-panties sort. The one-night-stand kind.

Just like Billy Chisholm.

Sabrina wasn't making the same mistake her mother had. At this point in her life, she was done with *just sex*. When she invested herself in a man, it would be one who would—could—love her and only her. A man who wouldn't spend every Saturday night cruising the local honky-tonk, picking up women, propositioning them.

Eventually, that is.

At this point in her life, she was busy with her career, dedicated to making her online-dating service a huge success. She needed a big payoff so that she could pay off her student loans, get herself out of debt and get on with her life. As a serious journalist. The website would give her the financial stability she needed right now. That's why she was here in Lost Gun—for the money. Not to find a date, much less a one-night stand.

Especially a one-night stand.

Sabrina didn't do one-nighters. And she most certainly didn't do cowboys.

Not now. Not ever.

No matter how much she suddenly wanted to.

HER CAR WOULDN'T START. The truth sank in after Sabrina cranked the engine a record ten times, until the loud grumble turned into a faint series of clicks that filled her with a sense of dread.

It wasn't the first time it had happened. The car was over ten years old. A clunker she'd inherited from her grandfather before leaving town all those years ago. While she did her best to keep up the oil changes and take care of her one and only means of transportation, she'd found herself stranded here lately more times than she could count. She needed a new car. Even more, she needed the money to afford a new car. She rested her forehead on the wheel and cursed the pile of junk for several seconds before gathering her resolve and popping the hood. Outside, she lifted the heavy metal, grabbed a rag she kept stashed in the front grill and started checking her battery connections.

Corrosion had built up and she damned herself for not shelling out the hundred bucks to buy a new one before leaving L.A. But she was on a budget. One that barely allowed for the secondhand shoes on her feet and the designer skirt she'd picked up at a thrift store in Hollywood. Clothes that made her feel like a million bucks even though her bank account reflected anything but. Still. If she'd learned anything from marketing guru Livi, it was that success was all about projecting a certain image. About building a brand.

And her brand as a high-powered executive for the next big website did not involve shoving her face under a hood and praying for divine intervention.

She thought about going back inside and hunting down Livi. Her friend, never short on cash thanks to a decent trust fund from her parents, had picked up her own rental car when they'd arrived in town so that they could split up and cover more territory. The rental wasn't anything extravagant—this was Lost Gun, after all—but it ran. They'd met here at the kick-off dance after Sabrina had spent the day at the fairgrounds while Livi had visited a nearby working ranch rumored to employ the hottest ranch hands in the entire county. Livi would give her a lift back to their motel.

Sabrina weighed her options. Calling or texting were both out because Livi was notorious for ignoring her phone when in the arms of a hot, hunky man. That meant Sabrina would have to go back inside and risk running into Billy Chisholm again.

She ditched the idea and fiddled a few more minutes with the connections. Sliding behind the wheel, she cranked the engine again.

Click. Click. Click.

"It's flooded," Billy's deep voice slid along her nerve endings and put her entire body on instant alert. He leaned down, his handsome face filling up the driver's window. The scent of clean soap and raw, sexy male teased her nostrils. "I hate to break it to you, but you're not going anywhere anytime soon."

She blew out an exasperated breath and reached for her cell phone. "I guess it's time to call a tow truck."

"Good luck."

She eyed him. "What's that supposed to mean?"

"That there's only one tow truck in town, sugar, and it belongs to George Kotch," he murmured as if that explained it all. When she didn't seem the least bit enlightened, he added, "He's about a hundred years old and tires out real easy." He glanced at his watch. "It's already after ten. By now, he's already eaten his bowl of ice cream, taken out his dentures and called it a night. Hell, he's probably been asleep a good five hours or so."

"Lovely," she muttered.

"On the bright side, he's up at the crack of dawn. He'll surely have you out of here and over at the filling station by the time they open. You'll get first dibs in the garage."

"Lucky me. What about a cab service?"

He shook his head. "Red's got a thing for TV. Started with soap operas and progressed to late night TV."

"Good Samaritan?"

His grin was slow and extremely sexy. "At your service."

"You want to give me a ride?"

His grin grew wider. "In the worst way."

"Why do I get the feeling you're talking about more than just driving me somewhere?"

"Because I am." His expression grew serious and his eyes glittered. "I want you and I'd bet my next buckle that you feel the same even if you don't seem all that anxious to admit it." He glanced around at the parking lot full of cars. Yet there wasn't a soul around. Everyone was back inside, dancing and drinking it up. "Seems like fate if you ask me. You run off in a tiff and bam, the car won't start. Maybe someone upstairs is trying to tell you that I'm not such a bad guy."

"No, you're a cowboy." Which was worse. Much worse.

At the same time, there did seem something almost inevitable about the way he'd shown up right when she needed a hand. That, and he was right. She did want him. More than she wanted her next breath. Her last relationship had been nearly a year ago and she'd been flying solo ever since. She craved a little physical contact in the worst way. So much so that she found herself thinking about him and the way he smiled and smelled and looked so indescribably good. And all when she should have been thinking about the website and how they were going to make their quota.

Yep, she had a craving, all right. One that wasn't going to go away unless she satisfied it in a major way.

"I'm staying at the Lost Gun Motel," she heard herself murmur.

Something dark and dangerous and oh so mesmerizing sparked in his violet eyes. "Well, what do you know? So am I." He opened the car door. "My pickup's just right down the row." His grin faded and a look of pure determination carved his expression. "Let's go."

Warning bells clamored in her head, but the only thing she seemed conscious of was the frantic beat of her heart.

The excitement.

The anticipation.

The need.

"Just so we're clear," she managed to say despite the heat zipping up and down her spine, "this is just sex. We won't be exchanging phone numbers or going out on a date or anything like that."

He nodded. "That's the last thing I want."

"I'm not interested in getting to know you as a person. This is just physical."

He nodded. "Purely physical."

She squelched an unexpected rush of disappointment at his words and concentrated on the trembling in her hands and the desire coiling in her belly. "Then lead the way."

4

BILLY CHISHOLM'S HANDS actually trembled as he shoved the key into the lock of the Lost Gun Motel, a clean but ancient establishment just off the main strip of town. It had been a long, long time since he'd been this worked up. This hot. This hard. This...anxious.

The knowledge would have been enough to send him running for the next county if the circumstances had been different—if Sabrina had been any of the dozens of marriage-minded women who'd been in hot pursuit since his oldest brother had found the love of his life and gone off the market.

Now Billy was the resident bad boy, which wasn't a bad thing on account of he liked being bad. He liked making noise and breaking rules and living life.

He liked the rush from all three.

At one time, so did every available woman in town. The trouble was, where they'd once wanted a good time back in high school, they now wanted a walk down the aisle. Marriage. *Kids*.

They wanted Billy Chisholm to grow up, man up and settle down, and each and every one thought she'd be the one to make it happen. To rope, tie and tame him before he knew what was happening.

Not this cowboy.

He liked being single. Hell, he loved it. He didn't have to answer to anyone. To worry about anyone. To hurt anyone.

He was the offspring of the most irresponsible man in the county. Silas Chisholm had been a two-bit criminal who'd pulled off the most impressive heist in the county, before pissing it away because of a case of white lightning and a lit cigarette. And all without a thought for his three young sons. The man had been selfish. Unpredictable. Unreliable.

Bad to the bone.

And out of all three boys, Billy was just as bad.

But while he looked like Silas, and even acted like him on occasion, he also knew what it felt like to be on the receiving end of someone else's bad decisions, and so he'd made up his mind to never, ever put someone else in that position. The last thing Billy Chisholm would ever do was get himself lassoed by any one woman.

Even one as hot and sexy as this one.

But Sabrina Collins didn't want to marry him. With her high heels and tasteful clothes and reluctant demeanor, she was as far removed from Lost Gun as a woman could get. She had big city written all over her, even if she did drive a clunker. Even more, she was a stranger. A single stranger. And judging by the way she licked her lips, she wanted the same thing from him that he wanted from her—sex.

He pushed open the door, stepped back and let her precede him inside. He expected more of an exotic fragrance from her, given her big-city appearance and the whiff of cotton candy he'd caught back at the dance courtesy of the flowing martinis. The scent had long since disappeared. Instead, the warm scent of apples and cinnamon filled his nostrils as she eased past him. She smelled like sweet, fresh-from-the-oven apple pie, and his nostrils flared. A warning sounded somewhere in the back of his brain, but it wasn't loud enough to push past the sudden hammering of his heart. A bolt of need shot through his body and his muscles bunched. He barely resisted the urge to haul her into his arms, back her up against the wall and take her hard and fast right there under the bare porch light, the june bugs bumping overhead.

He fought the crazy urge because Billy Chisholm didn't do fast and furious. He didn't lose his head where women were concerned. He stayed firmly in the saddle, calm and controlled.

Laying a woman down on a soft mattress, peeling away the clothes one piece at a time and taking things slow. That was the way to go. The way he always went, because losing his head wasn't part of the proposition. A man said things he didn't mean when he lost his head.

He followed her inside, closing the door behind them. A click sounded as she turned on a nearby lamp. A pale yellow glow pushed back the shadows and illuminated the interior. The room was far from fancy, but it was neat and clean. An unfinished pine dresser sat in the far corner, an ancient-looking television rested on top. A king-size bed took up the rest of the space. Calico curtains covered the one window near a window air-conditioning unit. A matching comforter draped across the bed. The slightly scarred hardwood floor gleamed from a recent polishing. He had his own place outside of town—just a small cabin he'd been building over the past year—but during rodeo time he hated to waste his time driving back and forth, and so he'd opted to rent a room here.

"It's not the Crown Plaza, but it should do."

"I've never stayed at the Plaza." She licked her lips again and he had the gut feeling that she'd never done this sort of thing before. And then his gaze caught hers and he knew deep down that this was, indeed, a first for her.

Not a one-night stand. No, she seemed to know her way around when it came to that.

The first had more to do with him. She'd never done this with a man like him before.

"You're not usually into cowboys, are you?"

"Never." His blood rushed even faster at her admission. A crazy reaction because Billy wasn't in the habit of being the first anything when it came to women. Be it the first cowboy or the first one-night stand or the first man to actually cause an orgasm. Rather, he steered clear of any situation that might set him apart in a woman's mind and make him more than just a really good lay.

He stiffened, his fingers tightening on the room key. "Maybe this isn't such a good idea."

"You're right about that." The hesitant light in her gaze faded into a wave of bright blue heat as she stepped closer. "It's not good at all." Another step and her nipples touched his chest. "You're so *not* my type."

Before he could blink, she shifted things into high speed, pressed herself against him and thrust her tongue into the heated depths of his mouth, kissing him, devouring him, shaking his sanity and his precious control.

Before he could think, his body reacted. His hands went to her tight, round ass, and he pulled her even closer. He rubbed his throbbing erection against the cradle of her pelvis. His fingers bunched material until he reached the hem of the skirt and felt her bare flesh beneath. Her thighs were hot to the touch. Soft. Quivering.

Holy shit.

Urging her backward, he eased her down onto the bed. He captured her mouth in a deep, intense kiss that lasted several heartbeats before he pulled away and stepped back. He drew a much-needed breath, determined to get himself in check and hop back into the driver's seat. He pulled his T-shirt over his head and tossed it to the floor. He unfastened the button on his jeans and pushed the zipper down. The pressure eased and the edges gaped and he could actually breathe for a few seconds.

Until she pushed to a sitting position and leaned forward.

Her fingers touched the dark purple head of his erection where it pushed up above the waistband of his briefs. The air lodged in his throat and he ground his teeth against a burst of white-hot pleasure. Her touch was so damn soft and he was so hard and...

He needed to touch her.

To see her.

He reached for the hem of her blouse and pulled it up and over her head. One dark nipple pushed through the lace-patterned cup of her black bra. He leaned over and flicked his tongue over the rock-hard tip. She gasped and he drew the nub deeper into his mouth, sucking her through the flimsy covering.

Her fingers threaded through his hair and held him close. He relished the taste of her flesh for several heart-pounding moments before he pulled away. He gripped the cups of her bra and pulled them down and under the fullness of her breasts. The bra plumped her and her ripe nipples raised in invitation.

When he didn't lower his head and suckle her again, she reached for him. "What are you waiting for?"

"Easy, darlin'. We'll get to it." But not yet. He meant to take his time. He always took his time and now was no different.

She was no different.

Even if she was softer and warmer and sweeter than any woman he'd ever been with.

He unzipped her skirt and peeled it from her body

in a slow, tantalizing motion that stirred goose bumps in her soft flesh. Trailing his fingers back up the way they'd come, he hooked his fingers at the thin straps of her panties and followed the same path down her long legs. When he had her naked, with the exception of the bra pulled beneath her luscious breasts, he leaned up and let his gaze sweep the length of her.

She was definitely not from around here, he realized when his attention settled on the barely-there strip of pubic hair that told him she'd been waxed at some big-city salon rather than the local Hair Saloon.

"Did you get this back in L.A.?" He trailed a finger down the barely-there strip of hair and watched her tremble.

"Yes."

"I like it." He traced the slit that separated her lush pink lips and a groan trembled from her mouth. Her legs fell open and the soft pink flesh parted for him.

He dipped his fingertip into her steamy heat and watched her pupils dilate. Her mouth opened and she gasped. And then he went deeper, until her eyes fluttered closed and her head fell back. He worked her, sliding his finger in and out until her essence coated his flesh and a drop trickled over his knuckle.

Hunger raged inside him and he dipped his head, flicked his tongue over the swollen tissue and lapped up her sweetness.

At the first contact of his mouth, she arched up off the bed and her hands tangled in his hair. He tasted her, savoring the bitter sweetness and relishing the soft, gasping sounds coming from her trembling lips. He swirled his tongue around her clitoris and felt the tip ripen for him. She whimpered as he sucked the sensitive nub into his mouth and nibbled until she tensed beneath him. Her fingers clutched at his hair in a grip that was just short of painful. The sensation fed his ravenous desire and made his breath quicken. He stroked her once, twice and her breath caught on a ragged gasp.

"Please. Just do it. Do it now."

He gathered his control and pulled away, determined to make it last for both of them. But then his gaze collided with hers and he saw the fierce glitter in her eyes—a mix of desire and impatience and fear—and he had the strange feeling that there was more than just an orgasm hanging in the balance.

As if she feared the morning after even more than he did.

Good.

At least they were both on the same page.

That meant if one of them lost perspective for whatever reason, the other could push them back on track. It was all about tonight.

This moment.

Nothing more. He snatched up his jeans and retrieved a condom from his pocket. After sliding on the latex, he settled between her legs. Bracing himself, he shoved his penis deep into her wet heat in one swift thrust that stalled the air in his lungs.

He gripped her lush hips, his tanned fingers digging into her pale flesh as he plunged into her again.

She closed her eyes, lifted her hips and met each thrust until he couldn't take it anymore. His cock throbbed and filled and he was right there. He thrust again and the pressure built.

Pleasure fogged his brain and before he could stop himself, he reached down between them and parted her flesh just above the point where he filled her. He caught her swollen clitoris between his thumb and forefinger and squeezed lightly.

She moaned and her body convulsed around him and he knew she'd tumbled over the edge. He buried himself deep one last time and followed. He held her tight and relished the way her inner muscles milked him.

Finally, his hold loosened and he collapsed onto his back. He reached for her, tucking her against his body and losing himself in the frantic pounding of his heart.

Fear hammered at the edges of his brain, but he wasn't going to let it in. Not just yet.

There would be plenty of time later to beat himself up over the fact that he'd lost control for a few precious seconds and, in the process, violated every promise he'd ever made to himself when it came to women and sex.

Plenty of time.

But right now… Right now he just wanted to close his eyes and hold her close. Just for a little while.

Get up. That's what Sabrina told herself the minute she heard the soft snores coming from the man next to her.

Get up.

Get out.

Get moving.

While she didn't have to worry about alarming Livi if she failed to make it out of Billy's room before day-break—she and Livi had opted to get separate rooms since they were splitting up most of the time to work more territory—she'd still promised to meet her first thing in the morning for breakfast.

Even more, she had a column to finish for one of the blogs she regularly wrote for. The name of the col-umn? "Oh, No, She Didn't." It was a weekly tell-all on female celebrities and their outlandish behavior that she penned for a tabloid website out of Los Angeles. A far cry from CNN or Fox News, but the site paid a small fee per word and at least she was actually getting paid to write something. Heaven knew she had a stack of journalism pieces she'd written on spec that would never see the light of day. Commentaries on the state of the nation, a story on the outrageous salaries paid by the L.A. County Water Department, and even a twenty-page analysis on the anti-gluten craze. Anything she'd felt might draw some interest, she'd penned and sent in to every newspaper and website she could think of. And the most she'd gotten back was a few comments saying her writing was good, but they needed material that was groundbreaking. A fresh angle. A cutting edge story that would sell copy. And so she'd stuck with her one sure writing gig—the column for the tabloid site. A paycheck, however small, at least made her dream seem legitimate, even if it didn't pay the bills.

She thought of the bank robbery that had put Lost

Gun on the proverbial map. The story had been big news back in the day, but she didn't know nearly as much as she needed to in order to start thinking about an angle. An easy fix, of course, thanks to Google. A few articles would put her up to speed and maybe spark some ideas for a new look at the story. But first she needed facts.

Who? What? When? Where?

Billy's arms tightened around her and suddenly the last thing she wanted to do was spend the rest of her night chained to her computer, checking facts or slogging another story about yet another actress who'd ditched rehab and gone on a party spree.

No, what she really wanted was to stay right here and snuggle down into the warmth wrapped around her.

All the more reason to get up.

The last thing she needed was to fall asleep and risk an awkward morning after. While she'd fallen out of practice thanks to her change of heart, she'd still had enough one-night stands to know that she didn't want to get stuck facing Billy Chisholm the morning after.

She had no doubt he would tell her thanks and hit the road faster than she could blink. He'd made his intentions crystal clear, and so had she. She didn't want more. At least, not from him.

Now if he'd been any other man…

Maybe a bank executive or a photojournalist or anyone but a Stetson-wearing bull rider. Then she might have thought about getting to know him.

But she already knew more than enough.

Billy Chisholm wasn't her type.

She knew that, but with him so close, the scent of sexy male filling her head, she had the gut feeling that she wouldn't be all that happy to see him go.

The thought struck and she gave herself a mental kick. She didn't have to think about him walking out because she intended to walk out first.

Soon.

At the same time, it had been such a long day and she really was worn out. Exhausted. Might as well take advantage of the warmth and close her eyes for just a few seconds. A cat nap.

Then she was up and out of there.

Guaranteed.

5

"WHERE THE HELL are you?" Livi's frantic voice carried over the line the minute Sabrina answered her cell phone. "You're not hurt, are you? Oh, crap, you're not dead, are you?"

"Yes, and I'm speaking to you from the hereafter."

"Very funny. Seriously, I all but freaked when I woke up this morning and realized you hadn't come back to the motel room."

"Morning?" Sabrina blinked against the blinding light pouring through the open curtains, and panic seeped through her. It *was* morning.

She'd slept with Billy Chisholm.

Slept slept.

There'd been no creeping out before dawn. No "Thanks, but gotta go." Or "I really appreciated it, but have a nice life." No, she'd snuggled right up next to him and closed her eyes and now the sun was up and she was late.

"*So?*" Livi's voice pushed past the panic beating at her senses. "How was it?"

"How was what?" She glanced at the clock on the night-stand. It was eight-thirty in the morning. Not only had she fallen asleep, but she'd slept past her usual 7:00 a.m. And all because of a man.

A cowboy.

"Did you get lucky?"

More like *un*lucky. Of all the available men in town—the reporters and the out-of-town fans—she'd hooked up and fallen asleep with a homegrown, certi-fied, grade A *cowboy.*

"Well?" Livi prompted.

"I really need to go."

A thought seemed to strike and her friend's voice rose an octave. "You're not still with him, are you?"

Was she?

Her gaze ping-ponged around the room, looking for boots or clothes or *something* before stalling on the open bathroom door. She strained her ears for some sound, but there was no water running. No footsteps. Just the distant sound of a vacuum cleaner humming from a few rooms down.

"Of course not." She ignored the disappointment that niggled at her, pushed the blankets to the side and scrambled from the bed. She grabbed her undies, which lay on the floor a few feet away. "I'll meet you in a few minutes. Where are you?"

"The diner next door to the motel, remember? That's where we agreed to meet."

"Oh, yeah."

"Cowboys have to eat, right?" Livi went on. "Plus, they've got the best coffee in town and you know how I need my coffee. Lots of coffee."

"Save a few cups for me. I'll be there in ten."

She spent the next few minutes plucking her clothes up off the floor and damning herself for forgetting the all-important fact that she'd agreed to a one-night stand only. The key word being *night*. She'd had every intention of being the first one to hit the road after the deed had been done, the first one saying goodbye, walking out, calling the shots.

She certainly hadn't meant to close her eyes. To get too comfortable. To forget for even a split second that cowboy Billy was not the morning-after type and that, even more, neither was she.

Luckily that all-important fact hadn't slipped *his* mind.

She spared a quick glance around the room. There was no suitcase. No personal items scattered across the dresser. No clothes hanging in the closet. And definitely no note. He'd taken everything with him as if he meant to never come back.

And the problem is?

No problem. Sure, she preferred being the one out the door first, but at least he'd had the good sense not to linger and make things that much more awkward.

Anxiety pushed her that much faster and she pulled on her clothes quickly. She was getting out of here now, and she wasn't going to think that maybe, just maybe, it might have been nice if he'd at least said goodbye.

Forget worrying over one measly cowboy. She had one hundred and fifty-two to think about.

Slipping out of the motel room, she ignored the knowing smile on the maid's face as she rushed down the walkway and rounded the corner toward her own room. A quick shower and change, and she would hit the soda machine next to the ice maker before the diner. She wasn't facing Livi and a room full of Stetsons until she'd calmed down completely. To do that, she needed sugar. Lots of sugar.

A soda. Maybe a bag of M&Ms.

Forget a fully stocked minibar for the source. The Lost Gun Motel was like any other small-town inn she'd ever known.

That meant vending machines instead of minibars. Homegrown soda fountains and pharmacies instead of McDonald's or a CVS. A family-owned general store instead of the brand-name, big-box type.

Sure enough, she rounded another corner and spotted an old Coke machine stuffed with glass-bottled sodas. A crate sat next to the rusted-out monster, the slots half filled with empties.

Her gaze snagged on an Orange Crush and she could practically taste the sugary sweetness on her tongue. As if it had been just yesterday that she'd given up her favorite drink, instead of eight years. The day she'd turned eighteen and left town in her granddaddy's ancient Bonneville.

She'd never looked back since.

She'd never wanted to.

The soda had been just as bad for her as the small-minded hometown where she'd grown up, and so giving it up had been a no-brainer. She'd switched to lattes and bright lights and a great big city full of zillions of people who didn't know what a big pile of unreliability her father had been. There were no knowing looks when she walked into the corner drugstore. No one gossiping behind her back when she went into the nearest Starbucks. In L.A. she was just one of the masses, and she liked it that way. She liked her privacy.

Which was why she'd stayed away from home all these years.

Since her mother had dropped the bomb that she was getting married—again—to a local wrangler from one of the nearby ranches, despite the fact that she'd walked that road once before. Arlene had obviously learned nothing the first time with Sabrina's father. He'd been a ranch hand. Worth his salt when it came to horses, but worthless when it came to being a good husband and father. He'd cheated on her for years before finally running off with a barmaid from the local honky-tonk when Sabrina had been thirteen.

Her mother had been devastated. She'd cried for months, then she'd spent the next few years telling herself that he was coming back, that it was just temporary. Eventually, she'd faced the truth. Not that it had done any good. She'd turned around and hooked up with loser number two. Different time. Different man. Same story.

Sabrina hadn't been in any hurry to watch a repeat of the past. When her eighteenth birthday had rolled around, she'd packed up and left her mother, her mother's new cowboy and her small-town life in the dust.

Her resentment toward Arlene and her cheating father had faded over the years, but she'd never been able to bring herself to go home. To the same double-wide where she'd listened to her mother cry herself to sleep night after night after Sabrina's father had walked away. The place had never felt like home.

It never would, so there was no sense rushing back and pretending. Instead, she'd accepted the truth and turned her back on Sugar Creek like a piece of gum that had lost its flavor.

Sure, she'd seen her mother a few times over the years, but always on neutral ground. Arlene had flown out to California once. They'd met in Vegas another time. Colorado for Christmas a few years back.

She'd heard through the grapevine that her father had ended up single again, working on a horse ranch in Montana. Not that she cared. The day he'd walked away from her had been the day that he'd died in her mind, and so she had no desire to see him.

But as much as she hated him, she owed him, as well. He'd at least taught her one important thing—to never, ever fall for the same type of man.

A man who didn't know the meaning of the word *commitment*.

Which was why she was chalking last night up to a

good time. A temporary good time that was now over and done with.

No matter how much it had felt otherwise.

She slipped inside her motel room and spent the next few minutes getting dressed, before she heard a knock on the door.

"Maid service," came the voice from the other side a split second before the hinges creaked and the knob twisted. A woman with bleached-blond hair and too much red lipstick came up short in the doorway. "It's nearly noon," the woman said as she noted the towel wrapped around Sabrina. "Folks are usually up and about by now."

Folks, as in the locals. But Sabrina wasn't a local, which meant she fell into the same class as a communist/ sociopath/deviant puppy kicker. Small towns like Sugar Creek and Lost Gun were close-knit. Folks didn't take too kindly to outsiders, and they certainly didn't trust them. Which was why Sabrina made a point to give Olive—according to the name tag—a big smile before retreating to the bathroom to get dressed, and an even bigger tip when she grabbed her purse to leave fifteen minutes later. Not that it made her any less of a communist/sociopath/deviant puppy kicker. It just meant that she wouldn't have to beg for an extra set of towels. And maybe, just maybe, she might get an additional name or two to pursue for her database.

"So he's the hottest single male in town?" she asked Olive a few minutes later, after complimenting her lipstick and matching nail polish, and slipping her another five.

The woman shrugged as she smoothed Sabrina's sheets. "I don't know about hot, honey, but Martin Trawick is surely single, now that his fifth divorce is final, that is."

"He's been married five times?" Unease rolled through her.

"Six, actually, but we don't count the first one on account of it was old man Talley who officiated and he ain't an actual clergyman. Just tells folks that so's he can get the clergyman's discount special at the diner. It's an olive-loaf sandwich with fresh pickle chips. Anyhow, Martin is always looking for his next wife. He'd probably be tickled to sign up for your service."

Okay, he wasn't prime grade A marriage material. At the same time, they weren't promoting an actual *marriage* service. She and her roommates had invested a lot of time in their mission statement, which outlined their venture—namely, an interactive website where women could go to meet, not marry, cowboys. Which meant the only criteria she had to establish was that any prospective candidate was a Wrangler-wearing, cowboy-hat-tipping, boot-stomping country boy.

"What does Martin actually do for a living?"

"Owns a pecan farm outside town. Actually, he owns a sixth of the pecan farm on account of he had to split it with each of his exes, but he's still got a good hundred acres of his own."

Okay, he wasn't a pro bull rider, but he *was* country. *Check.*

"Does he wear boots?"

"You're in Lost Gun, sugar. Who doesn't wear boots?"

Check.

"How about a cowboy hat?"

"I reckon when he's out tending pecans and it's hot."

Check.

Sabrina smiled. "Where can I find him?"

6

"Now, THAT'S WHAT I'm talking about!"

Eli let loose a loud whoop as Billy climbed to his feet and dusted off his backside. Meanwhile, several wranglers chased the bull he'd just ridden for eight seconds toward the gate leading to the holding pen.

"If you ride like that in the semifinals on Saturday, you're sure to zip straight through to the finals."

If.

The word hung in the air because as much as Billy's pride told him he was a shoo-in, he knew better. While he knew he had the talent, other factors came into play when it came to a successful ride. With all the publicity from the *Famous Texas Outlaws* episode, Billy had been tense. Sleep deprived. Anxious. Even if he was damn good at hiding it.

Still, his numbers had been down in the preliminaries and while he'd had a good ride, good wasn't enough.

To make it to the Lost Gun finals, he had to be great.

And to make it all the way to the finals in Vegas in November?

He had to be flawless.

"That was damn near perfect," Eli said as he clapped Billy on the back and followed him out of the corral. Die-hard fans packed the training facility and cameras flashed left and right.

"Way to go, Billy!"

"Awesome ride!"

"You're the best!"

The comments came at him from all angles and fed the excitement already pumping through his veins.

Not that Billy was letting the praise go to his head. He knew that the past eight seconds meant nothing if he couldn't pull it off again on Saturday in front of the judges. That meant the next week of practice had to be this good. Or better.

Fat chance.

The doubt trotted into his head before he could close the gate, and unease settled low in his belly. Not because his success just now had anything to do with a certain brunette. Sure, the sex had relieved his tense muscles and given him the best sleep he'd had in a helluva long time, but she could have been anyone.

"Whatever you did last night, you better make damn sure you do it again." Eli retrieved a bottled water from a nearby cooler and handed it to Billy. "Rinse and repeat, buddy. Rinse and repeat."

If only.

He ignored the crazy thought and made his way

around the chutes toward the cowboy who waited on the other side of the railing.

His brother Jesse wore a serious expression that said *major badass*.

But Billy wasn't the least bit intimidated. At six foot three, Jesse had only an inch and a half on him. And when it came to attitude? Billy put the *b* in badass.

"Not too shabby," Jesse remarked when Billy reached him. "I might have taught you something, after all." He grinned and his violet eyes twinkled.

The same eyes that stared back at Billy in the bathroom mirror every morning. But while they had the same eyes and a similar build, that's where the likeness ended. Billy had sun-kissed blond hair, an easy smile and a shitload of Southern charm.

Jesse, not so much.

He'd always been the serious one, sick of his past and eager to leave it behind for something bigger and better. Which was why it had surprised everyone when Jesse had announced last week that he was not only staying in Lost Gun permanently but rebuilding on the old property that had once housed the one-room shack where they'd grown up.

The reason for his sudden change of heart?

The petite blonde standing on the opposite side of the corral, snapping pictures of the various bulls and riders as they exited the chute.

Jesse and Gracie Stone had had a thing for each other back in high school. A fire that had burned so fierce and bright that neither time nor a blanket of stubbornness had managed to smother. They'd kept their distance up until a few weeks ago when Gracie had warned Jesse about the renewed interest in Silas and the "Where Are They Now?" episode that had been about to air. One face-to-face and *bam,* the flames had reignited and blazed that much hotter. They were inseparable now. They'd moved into Gracie's house over on Main Street while they built their very own place on the ruins of Silas Chisholm's old house.

The news couldn't have come a moment too soon for Billy. While Jesse had been eager to forget the past, Billy had always been more inclined to remember.

To keep in mind the unreliable man his father had once been, and even more, to keep a tight hold on the man he knew lurked deep inside himself.

"You're my blood," he'd heard Silas say too many times to count. *"Just 'cause you think you're so high and mighty, don't make it true. You'll see. I ain't cut out for the nine-to-five life, and neither are you. There are too many options out there. Too many ways to make it really big to waste your time with some penny-ass job."*

The words had been spoken to Jesse, who'd been thirteen at the time and the caretaker to his two younger brothers, but Billy had been the one to take the statement to heart.

Silas Chisholm had never been able to settle down and straighten up his life. There'd been no finding a steady job and building a home for his boys and meeting a nice woman to share his life with. He'd been a lowlife who'd floated from one two-bit crime to the next, always looking for the next big thing. A better opportunity. A bigger payoff.

Ditto for Billy.

Not the crime, part. Hell, no. He was one hundred percent legit and damn proud of it.

It was his inability to commit in his personal life that made him a chip off the old block. It had started back in kindergarten when he hadn't been able to choose between the monkey bars and the slide, and continued through middle school—baseball or football?—and high school, where he'd accepted not one, but four invitations to his senior prom.

Even now, he couldn't seem to pick a shade of blue for the tile in his new bathroom, or figure out whether to add an extra bedroom to the cabin or a man cave. He could see the value in both, the payoff, and that was the problem. Billy hated to narrow his options. To miss out on something better. To *commit*.

Now, bulls were different.

They were the only thing he managed to focus on, to follow through with, to go balls to the wall without a second thought. A championship was the one thing he wanted with a dead certainty that he'd never felt for anyone or anything.

Until last night.

He nixed the crazy thought and ignored Eli's voice echoing in his ear. *"Rinse and repeat."*

Like hell.

He'd made it out of the motel room this morning without a confrontation or the dreaded "Call me, okay?"

Uh, no.

Last night had been just that—*last* night. *One* night. End of story.

"If you ride like that in the semifinals," Jesse went on, drawing his full attention, "you just might land yourself a spot in the final round."

"There's no *if*, bro," Billy said with his usual bravado. "I *will* ride like that. That purse is mine, and so is your title."

"I hope so, but all the positive affirmation can't change the past few days and the fact that you sucked big-time in the first go-round." Jesse shook his head. "What the hell happened?"

"I was running on fumes. Tired. Stressed. You know how it is."

"And now?"

Billy shrugged. "I finally got a decent night's sleep is all."

Jesse arched an eyebrow. "Jack Daniels or a double dose of Sleepy Time?"

"Don't I wish." Jesse arched an eyebrow and Billy shrugged. "You don't want to know. Listen, are you really serious about tonight?" He shifted the subject to the voice mail Jesse had left for him earlier that day. "You want me out at Big Earl Jessup's place?"

Jesse nodded. "At sundown. And if you see Cole, make sure you remind him. I left a voice mail, but he's got semifinals today in bucking broncs, so he probably hasn't checked his messages."

Billy eyed him. "You going to tell me what this is all about?"

"Tonight." Jesse motioned to the bull being loaded into a nearby chute. "You'd better get back to work." He winked. "You need all the practice you can get."

But it wasn't practice that Billy desperately needed.

He realized that as he spent the rest of the day busting his ass atop the meanest bulls in the county. His skill, his technique, his drive—it was all there. In spades. He'd just been too tired to shine.

No, what he *really* needed was another six hours of uninterrupted sleep courtesy of a certain brunette with a vibrant pink-and-white Hello Kitty tattoo on the slope of her left breast.

Not that he was admitting as much.

Any woman, he reminded himself. He'd been so hard up that any woman would have had the same effect.

And he knew just how to prove it.

"AND I WANT A MAN with dark hair and blue eyes. And he has to be at least six feet. And have all his own teeth. And no bunions. And I need him by next Saturday night, 7:00 p.m., sharp," announced the elderly woman who'd hobbled up to Sabrina's table at the Fat Cow Diner.

The woman wore her silver-white hair in a short bob, her round body stuffed into an aqua tracksuit and white tennis shoes. "The rodeo committee is hosting their Senior Sweetheart dance and I need a date," she went on. "They do it simultaneous with the bull-riding semi-finals on account of no one down at the senior center can watch the event on account of all the pacemakers and stents and they need every available EMS worker focused on the riders in case they get hurt. The name's Melba Rose Cummins, like the diesel engine but no relation. I'm a shoo-in for queen." She indicated the silver pin attached to the collar of her jacket. "I was princess last year and princess always wins queen second time around."

"Unless you're Shirley Hart," chimed in the woman standing next to her. She had the same silver-haired bob—a testimony to the weekly special over at the Hair Saloon—but she wore a hot-pink tracksuit that hung loosely on her thin frame. "Poor Shirley won princess six years in a row on account of she had bad eyesight and refused to wear her glasses onstage. Kept walking into the podium during evening wear and knocking over the mic stand, which totally killed her score. But she finally saved up her social security checks and got herself some of that fancy LASIK surgery." She shook her head. "Poor thing was so sure that seven would be her lucky number. But then she up and had a heart attack. Keeled over two weeks before the competition and that was that."

"Nobody wants to hear about poor Shirley," Melba said. "This is about me."

The pink track suit shrugged. "All's I'm sayin' is if that had been me and I woulda spent that kind of money, I would have made sure they had my eyes open when they laid me to rest. My name's Louise Talley, by the way."

"Here's the address where I need him to pick me up," Melba handed over a slip of paper that smelled like a mixture of mothballs and dry-cleaning fluid.

"I'm sorry," Livi started, "but we're not an escort service. We run a website for women looking to meet cowboys."

"I don't care if he's a cowboy as long as he's in good shape," Louise said.

"That's nice, but we can't guarantee someone to pick you up next Saturday night—"

"He can meet me there," Melba cut in. "Just make sure he wears a tie. He'll have to walk me across the stage." She reached for her white patent-leather purse. "Cash or credit?"

"We can't—" Sabrina started, but Livi held up a hand.

"Cash."

Melba unearthed a coin purse and stared at the two dollar bills inside. "I'm afraid I'll have to go to the ATM."

"We'll be here waiting."

"What are you doing?" Sabrina asked when the two old women had disappeared.

"Getting rid of them."

"But they'll come back."

"And we won't be here." She motioned to the waitress. "Check, please. This place is a dead end," she told Sabrina. "Let's head over to the rodeo grounds. Maybe we'll have better luck there."

"That seems kind of rude."

"You know what's rude? The fact that we've explained our business over a zillion times and we keep getting these ridiculous requests. It says right on the pamphlet—meet the cowboy of your dreams. Meet. Not date. Or marry. Or molest. All we do is set up a meet."

"Maybe we can at least find her a prospect before next week. The actual date would be up to him at that point."

"Are you kidding me? We've got bigger fish to fry. I only managed to snag three profiles this morning. That coupled with the two I picked up last night leaves one hundred and forty-seven more. At this rate, we'll be over a hundred shy by our deadline. We have to speed up, not slow down and play escort service for the Lost Gun seniors."

"You're right." But that didn't mean Sabrina wasn't going to at least keep her eyes open for a prospect. She told Melba Rose as much when she caught her coming out of the feed store next door, cash in hand. "I can't make any promises, but I'll try."

"That's good enough for me." Melba made to hand her the cash, but Sabrina waved it away. "If I come up with someone, you can pay the usual posting fee after the fact."

"Next Saturday at seven," Melba reminded her. "And I'm negotiable on the teeth."

"That's good to know."

7

"WHAT EXACTLY ARE we doing out here?" The question came from Cole, Billy's older brother, as they stood in the middle of a huge pasture located behind Big Earl Jessup's worn-looking house.

Big Earl was a throwback to the good old days when moonshine was just as much a commodity as the cattle grazing in the nearby pastureland. He'd gained notoriety for his white lightning moonshine and his eccentric method of cooking—namely in his deer blind.

Those days were long gone, however, and his great-granddaughter was now cooking up the family recipe in the nearby garage. At least that was the rumor circulating around town, along with several jars of premium, grade A liquor.

At ninety-three, Big Earl spent his days in front of the TV with a tube of Bengay to soothe his severely arthritic joints. He lived just outside of town on several acres guarded by the pair of pit bulls currently tied up on the front porch. The sun had just set and darkness blanketed the area. The only light came from the windows of Big Earl's house and the lantern in Jesse's hand.

"The money's here," Jesse announced.

Billy's curiosity piqued and he spoke up. "Silas buried it here?"

"Actually, Big Earl buried it out here. He was Dad's partner. A silent partner. It turns out that Big Earl was on the construction crew that built the savings and loan some fifty-five years ago. He knew the place like the back of his hand, but he was too old to actually pull off a heist. Instead, he planned the robbery and Dad executed it. The plan was to hide the money and lay low for a while before spending any of it. But then Dad died and they featured him in *Famous Texas Outlaws* and the time never seemed right, so Big Earl was afraid to dig up the money. And then his old-timer's set in and now he can't actually remember where he buried it. He knows it's somewhere out here, in the middle of a tall stretch of grass."

Billy glanced from side to side. "This pasture's a good twenty acres each way."

"I know. That's why I need you two to help. I can't cover all this ground by myself."

"Can I ask a dumb question?" Cole held up a hand. "Why don't we tell the sheriff and let them get out here and dig the money up? It's not like we had anything to do with it."

"No, but we might as well have. If we hand over the info to the sheriff, the entire town will think we knew all along. But if we give it back ourselves, maybe we can prove once and for all that we aren't anything like Silas Chisholm. He took from this town, and now we're going to give back." He tossed a shovel at Billy. "We're going to dig every night up and down this pasture until we hit pay dirt. It might take a few days. It might take a few months."

Billy shrugged. "I guess hauling an excavator up here would attract too much attention."

Jesse nodded. "If anyone gets wind that the money might be here, there will be gold diggers from here to Houston looking for that money. We have to keep this between us and do it ourselves."

"How long are we supposed to dig tonight?" Cole asked. "Not that I don't want to dig. I'm totally on board with the plan, I just didn't figure on being up here all night."

"Don't worry. You'll be out in time for a booty call. Which Barbie is it this time?"

"None." Cole shook his head. "Jimmy and Jake hooked up with Crystal and April and they're now officially off the market."

Jimmy and Jake Barber were the last two members of the Lost Boys. They were twins who competed on the team roping circuit. They'd always been players when it came to the ladies, but it looked as if they're carousing days were fast coming to a close.

"Jimmy and Jake are getting serious?" Billy arched an eyebrow.

"Last I heard," Cole replied.

"And what about Barbie sister number three?" Jesse

asked. "You thinking about making an honest woman of her?"

"Hardly. Nikki Barbie may look as good as her sisters, but she's not nearly as much fun." Cole shrugged. "Besides, I met someone today." He grinned. "A lot of someones. There are girls coming out of the woodwork at this rodeo and I aim to make the most of it."

Jesse eyed Cole. "Love at first sight?"

Billy grinned. "Safe to say it's lust at first sight."

Cole shrugged. "Lust is good."

Jesse motioned to Cole. "Don't worry, you won't miss your booty call." He turned to Billy. "What about you? You got a midnight rendezvous planned?"

If only.

Billy stifled the thought and gripped the shovel. "Let's just get this done." And then he started to dig.

"IF I SEE ANOTHER female, I'm going to slit my wrists," Livi said the next day as she collapsed in the chair next to Sabrina. It was Sunday—over twenty-four hours since she'd met Billy Chisholm on Friday night—and the fair was in full swing.

She stared at the crowds milling about the rodeo arena where they'd set up their booth. While there were plenty of single males walking here and there, none of them were falling all over themselves to fill out a profile. No line around the corner like the nearby funnel cake stand. No whoops and hollers like the kissing booth across the way. "This obviously isn't working. You man

the table and I'll go see if I can stir up some business."
She stood and grabbed a stack of flyers.

"Where are you going?"

"The animal pens. There are a ton of hands on duty
over there."

"They're all working. I doubt they'll want to stop to
fill out a questionnaire."

"They will if I'm offering an incentive." Livi pulled
a white bakery box from beneath the table.

"What are those?"

"Seductive Strawberry cupcakes. A lady over at the
diner makes them. The place was full of old geezers
from the local VFW hall all going nuts over these. There
was a line clear out the door. I figure if they can stir
up the old guys, they might help out with the younger
ones. I bought a full dozen. I'm thinking this will nab
at least twelve men. Twenty-four if we cut them in half."

"Five minutes and writer's cramp for half of a Seductive Strawberry cupcake. Sounds like a fair trade."

"Hey, I'm desperate. And desperate times call for
desperate measures. See what you can do to get more
men to stop here. Undo a few buttons." She motioned
to Sabrina's blouse. "Or hike up the skirt."

"Why don't I just strip down to my underwear and
do a table dance."

"Great, but make sure to peel off the granny panties
first." Livi winked and disappeared.

She was *not* doing a table dance. Not yet, at least.

She pulled out more flyers, grabbed her clipboard
and rounded the table. If she couldn't lure the remain-

ing one hundred and twenty-seven eligible cowboys still needed over to her table for information, she would take the information to them.

She spent the next hour walking the aisles and approaching every available man. And a few not-so-available ones who hadn't been wearing their wedding rings. She'd been cussed at (*Mrs.* Tammy Johnson, wife of thirty-something Max Johnson, whose three daughters were showing goats in the arena next door) *and* kicked (*Mrs.* Denise Carter, wife of Harley Carter, a professional steer wrestler and competition eater signing autographs over in the barbecue tent), and all in less than ten minutes.

"I'm really sorry," Sabrina called after the blonde as pain radiated up her calf. "He's not wearing a wedding ring."

"He doesn't have to. The entire town knows he's mine. Now you do, too."

"It was an honest mistake," she tried again, but the woman had already rounded the corner.

"Don't let Denise bother you," came a voice from behind. "She's got somewhat of a temper."

Sabrina turned to see a seventyish woman wearing a flower-print dress half covered with a pink apron, a large white box clutched in her hand. Her silvery-white hair was rolled into fat sausage curls and piled high on top of her head. A pair of pink bifocals sat low on her nose. The scent of rich chocolate and cheap hairspray filled the air. "Why, she once threw a package of fish sticks at old Mrs. Shivers for looking at Harley in the checkout line at the Piggly Wiggly. Almost gave her a concussion, too, since the frozen-foods cooler runs a good twenty degrees lower than it should on account of Mr. Ricks—he's the owner—is too cheap to get the darn thing fixed. Name's Sarah Jean Hunt," the woman said, hefting the box to one arm and holding out her hand. "I own Sarah's Sweets. It's the one and only bakery in town."

"Sabrina Collins. I'm with—"

"FindMeACowboy.com," Sarah Jean finished for her. "I heard. The whole town's heard. You guys are here to sign up cowboys for your new website. Talk about exciting stuff."

"Your town hosts one of the biggest rodeos in Texas and you were just featured in a *Famous Texas Outlaws* episode. I can't imagine a website start-up is big news."

"To me it is." The older woman drew a deep breath as if gathering her courage. "I'm here to sign up for your hook-up service."

"I'm afraid we've reached our quota on females. We're here in town to sign up more men."

"I know. That's why I brought these." She held up the bakery box. "I sell everything from pies to cream puffs, but cupcakes are my specialty. Your friend bought a dozen of my Seductive Strawberry 'cause all those geezers from the VFW hall like them. But they just like 'em 'cause the strawberry puree I use works better than their Metamucil. If you want to rope in the younger ones, you need to try my Frisky Fudge Fantasy. I use a dark chocolate guaranteed to rev the libido and make any man hornier than a buck during mating season."

"Dark chocolate does that?"

"My dark chocolate does that. Mix it up myself with a secret recipe handed down from my great-grandmother. She used to own a brothel at one time and it's been said the menfolk would come from miles around to sample her goodies. 'Course, most folks think *goodies* refers to something sexual, but I know better 'cause I got all her recipes. Anyhow, if you want to sign up the cowboys around here, just give 'em one of these." She handed over the bakery box. "And there's more where those came from. All I ask in return is that you help me hook up with my very own cowboy."

While Livi had seemed convinced about the cupcakes, Sabrina wasn't nearly as gullible. Not after getting her leg kicked in. "Listen, Miss Sarah, I'd love to help, but—"

"I know I ain't no spring chicken. That's why I need your help. See, I'm not the luckiest when it comes to men. Spent nearly twenty years with a drunk rat bastard who up and died on me and left me with three kids to raise and not one penny of life insurance. Went into business for myself doing the only thing I knew how. I made it, too. The thing is, on account of running my own business and raising my girls, I ain't never had much free time to get out and meet many men. And I ain't really trusted my own instincts after picking such a dud the first go-round." She motioned to Sabrina.

"But you could find me a decent guy. That's what you do, right? Your specialty?"

"Actually, I have a journalism major. Livi, my partner, is the marketing guru who actually designed the meet-and-greet system—"

"But you find the men, right?"

"Actually, we're both here to find the men. Our friend Kat helps out, too, but she's back in L.A. right now working on the website."

"A triple threat." Sarah Jean grinned. "I like it." Hope glimmered in her eyes. "So you and your partner help me, and I'll help you."

No.

That was her first instinct.

She needed to fill her database, not search for one man for one particular woman.

Then again, she wasn't filling anything at the moment. She eyed the whopping two profiles she'd managed to complete in almost as many hours, before shifting her gaze back to Sarah. That, and she'd already committed herself to Melba. What was one more?

The old woman wasn't the ideal twenty-thirty-something they specialized in. Still, she *was* a strong, successful female. Determined and forthright. And she had the whole Mrs. Fields thing going on. Definitely a prize catch for any man over the age of seventy-five.

Provided the men over seventy-five were fishing.

There was only one way to find out.

She smiled at the older woman. "You've got yourself a deal."

HE WAS HAVING shitty luck.

Billy came to that realization after a sleepless Saturday night spent tossing and turning and staring at the ceiling, followed by an exhausting Sunday spent busting his ass at every turn.

"You suck," Cole told him when he took time out from his broncs to watch Billy during a practice ride. "You'll never make it through the semifinals like that."

"That's what I've been telling him," Eli said. "What happened to yesterday? You were so good."

"I had a late night." A fruitless night spent digging for a bunch of money that may or may not exist. At least that was Billy's take on the situation. To top it off, he'd spent the morning at his cabin trying to narrow down the flooring choices for the new bathroom. Hardwood or tile? The question ate at him when he should have had his mind on his ride. He needed to make his mind up so that the contractor could actually finish a job that should have taken three weeks. Instead, they were on month number two. And all because Billy couldn't just pick one.

He could.

He would.

It's just that he liked both.

Just as he'd liked both blondes that had hit on him last night at the local bar. They'd both been attractive, sexy, eager. He could have had either one of them.

He should have had one of them.

Then he wouldn't be sucking so badly now.

That's what he told himself, but deep in his gut, he

knew it wasn't true. He'd slept on Friday night after the sexual encounter with Sabrina not because he'd needed sex, but because he'd needed sex with her. Because he didn't have to worry about the act coming back to bite him because he knew she was temporary.

She didn't want more and neither did he and he was through denying it.

He had to do something. Even if it went against his good judgment.

"Where are you going?" Eli asked when Billy picked himself up off the ground, dusted off his jeans and started for the gate. "You've still got a few hours left of practice."

"I'm tired of busting my ass. I need an insurance policy." And then he headed for the fairgrounds next door and the woman with the Hello Kitty tattoo.

8

SABRINA FOUGHT TO control the trembling in her hands as she headed down the aisle of booths and rounded the corner into the food section. The scent of sweet cotton candy called to her, but she was too determined to get as far away from Billy Chisholm as was humanly possible.

Sure, she'd been attracted to him last night. But that had been deprivation on her part and sexy mystique on his. But she'd explored that mystery in great detail. She'd climbed to the top of the mountain. She'd jumped off the ledge, and so it should have been downhill from there.

It was always downhill from there.

She shouldn't be trembling. Or shaking. Or wanting. Especially the *wanting*.

Hunger yawned deep in the pit of her stomach and she found herself digging out a wad of change for an extra-large cotton candy. A few sugary-sweet wisps melted on her tongue and a rush of *aaaah* went through her.

There. Hunger sated. Now she could think straight

and remember the all-important fact that Billy Chisholm was off-limits. Cowboy non grata. The more distance she kept between them the better.

"Hey, Sabrina, wait up." His deep voice rumbled behind her and she half turned to see him headed down the food aisle, his jeans molding to his body in all the right places.

"Gotta run." She picked up her pace and headed straight for the sign that said Ladies' Room up ahead.

"I want to talk to you."

"There's nothing to talk about. Just write it down on the sheet and I'll get everything entered into the computer. You'll be hooking up with women in no time."

He stopped, but his voice followed her. "Why are you so freaking scared to talk to me?"

The question rang in her ears, pricking her ego and the self-worth she'd fought so hard to cultivate all those years she'd watched her mother hide out in her room every time Sabrina's father had done her wrong. There'd been no confrontation. No standing up for herself. She'd taken it and retreated, and then she'd forgiven him and the pattern had started all over again.

She stopped dead in her tracks and turned on him. "Maybe I'm not scared. Maybe I just have nothing to say to you."

"But I have something to say to you."

"Maybe I'm not interested in talking to you." She tried to sound nonchalant, but it was next to impossible when she caught a whiff of his scent. The enticing aroma of leather and male and that unnameable something that made her think of soft cotton sheets and the moonlight peeking past the curtains of his motel room… Forget it. Forget him. Forget the night before last. *Forget.*

She tried for a steadying breath. "Look, I realize that you're very popular around here, but unlike the other females in this town—" she motioned to the group of women near the funnel cake stand, their gazes hooked on Billy "—I'm not interested in being one of your groupies."

"Really?"

"Really."

"You know what I think?"

"I couldn't care less."

"I think," he said, stepping toward her, "you're pushing me away on purpose because you really are scared."

"There goes that word again." She gathered her courage and focused every last ounce on holding her ground. Last night she hadn't been prepared to resist him, hadn't been armed against his sexy grin and his sparkling eyes and his honey-dripping drawl. But she was ready now.

Bring it on, cowboy. Bring. It. On.

"Walking away doesn't mean I'm scared," she said. "It means I'm just not interested."

"Is that so?" He stared at her, his eyes bright and mesmerizing. His lips hinted at the faintest of grins and his gaze dropped, peeling away her clothes and caressing every bare inch.

Her skin tingled and her heart stalled.

Okay, maybe she wasn't prepared for this.

For *him.*

She feigned a smile. "They call it a one-night stand for a reason. It means one night and it's over."

"I know what it means."

"Then stop stalking me."

"You don't have to be afraid."

"For the last time, I'm not afraid of you."

"Not me, sugar." He took another step, closing the distance between them. "Us." The word trembled in the air between them.

"There is no *us,* or did you miss the whole one-night-stand explanation?"

"We're good together."

"We *were* good together. That night. I was horny. You were horny. I'm no longer horny. So that's the end of it. And if you're looking for more, that's great. I'll get your profile entered into my system and I'm sure you'll find a zillion girls to hook up with. You might even find Miss Right—"

"I'm not looking for a wife. Or a relationship." He hesitated, as if suddenly unsure. Something tugged at her heart. "I slept for the first time in a long time, I actually slept for a few solid hours. Since sleep is imperative to a good ride, I was hoping we could work something out."

"Wait a second." She tried to process his words. "You want to have sex with me again because I put you to sleep?" Not because she'd rocked his world or did that little twist with her hips that had sent him to the moon and back. "*Sleep?* Seriously?"

"I know it sounds crazy, but you don't know how

worked up I've been. I haven't slept a solid three hours in weeks." He ran a hand through his hair and she noted the weary light in his eyes. "I've got the semifinals this weekend. If I have a good showing, that'll mean the finals." His gaze locked with hers. "I had the best practice of my life yesterday." He shrugged. "I figure the night before had something to do with it, so I want a repeat."

"So go forth and hook up again." She motioned to the group of women still gathered near the stand. "Take your pick."

He grabbed her arm and hauled her around the corner behind one of the shopping booths.

"What are you doing—" she started, the words drowning in the lump in her throat as he invaded her space.

"Taking your advice." He swung her around to face him. "I pick you."

She stared up at him, wishing he wasn't so tall, so handsome, so…close. "I'm not ripe for picking."

His eyes darkened and she realized she'd said the wrong thing…or the right thing, depending on the part of her doing the thinking. From the heat pooling between her legs, she'd bet money it wasn't her head.

"I'd say you're plenty ripe, sugar." His thumb grazed the nipple pressing against her blouse, and heat speared her. "Ripe *and* juicy, and damn near ready to burst."

"That's not what I meant." She fought for an extra breath to send a much-needed jolt of oxygen to her brain. "From what I've seen, there are dozens of women around here eager for a chance to help you out. Why don't you go make your offer to someone who might actually be interested?"

"Because they've all got one thing on the brain—a wedding ring. This is a small town, sugar. The local girls aren't thinking about having a good time. They're more worried about what time you're going to call them tomorrow. And whether or not you're going to ask them to the church picnic. And when you're going to order the ring and pick out the crystal."

"There's nothing wrong with a nice piece of Waterford."

"Except that I'm more a Dixie cup kind of guy."

"Meaning?"

"I don't want to lead anybody on. I'm busy and I'm not the least bit interested in an actual relationship."

"So make that clear up front."

"Been there and done that."

"And?"

"It lasted one week. The day before I was set to leave for a rodeo up in Montana, her daddy showed up with a shotgun and a preacher. He wanted me to make an honest woman of her."

"What did you do?"

"I told him no and now I can't fly without a strip search. I took two buckshot fragments in the ass."

"You did not."

"It was easier just to leave it in than let a surgeon dig it out." He shook his head. "One-night stands don't happen well in a small town. And since I don't have time to drive up to Austin, I'm stuck here."

"So you want to have sex with me again because I'm an outsider and I'm convenient."

"And damn sexy." He touched her then, skin to skin, the tip of one finger at her collarbone, and her heart jumped at the contact. "You're something when you get all worked up."

Before she could form a reply, he dipped his head and kissed her.

Billy Chisholm tasted even better than she remembered. Hotter. More potent.

His hand cupped her cheek, the other splayed along her rib cage just inches shy of her right breast, his fingers searing through the fabric of her blouse. His mouth nibbled at hers. His tongue slid wet and wicked along her bottom lip before dipping inside to stroke and tease and take her breath away.

Now, this…this was the reason she'd walked away from him a few minutes ago. Because she'd been a heartbeat shy of crawling over the table and pressing herself into his arms and begging for another kiss.

And Sabrina had no intention of begging any man for anything. Especially a too-big-for-his-britches cowboy with a sexy smile and purposeful lips. He was off-limits…

The thought faded as his fingers crept an inch higher, closer to her aching nipple, which bolted to attention, eager for a touch, a stroke, something—anything.

His fingers stopped, but his mouth kept moving, his tongue stroking, lips eating, hungry…so hungry. His intent was pure sin, and Sabrina couldn't help herself; a moan vibrated up her throat.

He caught the sound, deepening the kiss for a delicious moment that made her stomach jump and her thighs quiver, and left no doubt as to the power of the chemistry between them.

"I'm sorry about your ass, but I really don't think this is a good idea," she murmured, dazed and trembling when he finally pulled away.

He leaned in, his breath warm against her ear. "Actually, sugar, I think it's the best idea I've had in a hell of a long time." His words made her shake and quiver all the more.

Shaking? Quivering? Over a cowboy?

This cowboy, a voice whispered, that same voice that had warned her off him the minute she'd spotted him across the arena. The voice that had urged her to cut and run when he'd approached her table.

Because no way was Sabrina going to fall head over heels for a Stetson-wearing, Wrangler-rocking cowboy.

At the same time, it wasn't as though Billy had moved in next door and she had to resist temptation day in and day out for God knew how long. It was two weeks, and that was only if he made it to the finals. Fourteen days at the most.

She could keep her head on straight and her heart intact for two weeks, DNA be damned.

Sure, her mother had a weakness for cowboys, but she'd been stuck in Sugar Creek, surrounded by them. There'd been no way out for her mother, who'd worked a minimum-wage job all her life and so, of course, she'd fallen victim to Sabrina's father's charms.

His lies.

His conniving ways.

But Sabrina had a clear-cut exit plan with Billy. That, and she had obviously yet to make up for the past months of deprivation since her last relationship. It was the long, endless dry spell making her so hot for Billy Chisholm. She had no doubt. Once she made up for that deprivation, the attraction would fade and she would stop forgetting that he was the very type of man she *didn't* want. A little sex in this case would definitely do her good.

And a lot of sex would be even better.

"No strings attached, right? You're not going to expect me to make pancakes or hold your hand at the Dairy Freeze or iron your shirts?"

"I'm in training. That means lots of protein for breakfast and no ice cream. And I get all my shirts dry-cleaned." His gaze met and held hers. "We spend the nights together. That's it."

"And then you go your way and I go mine?"

"That's the plan."

"All right, then." Her gaze locked with his and her heartbeat kicked up a notch. "I'm in."

9

"EVERYONE, I'D LIKE to welcome a special guest to the Lost Gun Senior Center. This is Sabrina Collins. She's in town for the rodeo festivities," said the petite blonde who read the pitch Sabrina had handed her when Sabrina had walked into the sprawling brick building and asked to pass out some free T-shirts and mugs to the residents. "Miss Collins is here all the way from Los Angeles, California. She's here promoting her new website, FindMeACowboy.com."

A murmur went through the group of women that filled the small recreation room.

"I'd like to find me a cowboy, that's for sure," murmured an elderly woman with brightly colored red hair. She wore a flower-print pantsuit and bright white tennis shoes.

"You'll have to get in line behind me," said yet another woman. She had white hair and wore enough blue eye shadow to make a Vegas showgirl envious. "I've been widowed the longest, so I get first dibs."

"That's a lie, Dolores Rankin. I've got you beat by at least three days on account of I lost my Joe on Good Friday and your Milton didn't bite the dust until Easter."

"Joe slipped into a coma on Good Friday."

"Same thing."

"Is not."

"Is too."

"Now, now," said the blonde. "Let's try to be on our best behavior, ladies. We've got company." The woman, Susan Swanson, according to her badge, smiled and gave Sabrina an apologetic glance. Susan was the recreation coordinator for the center, as well as the head coach for the senior ladies' softball team, Old Chix with Stix. The last bit of info came from the brightly colored pink T-shirt she wore. The front depicted a swinging bat and the phrase *You're never too old to open up a can of whup ass,* while the back held the names and positions of the various team members.

"You just think your perm don't stink," said the redhead, "'cause you're a pitcher. But I'm one fastball away from knocking you out for good."

"You and what joint replacement?" Dolores arched one penciled-in eyebrow.

Red's face crinkled into a thousand tiny lines as she frowned. "What is that supposed to mean?"

"That you creak more than the rusted-out barn door on my old farm."

"I do not."

"Do too."

"Ladies," Susan chimed in again. "I'm sure Miss Collins didn't come here to listen to a bunch of bickering. She's got some freebies for us, isn't that right?" Sabrina nodded and Susan glanced at her watch.

"And cupcakes, too." Sabrina held up a bakery box, courtesy of Sarah and their newly formed alliance. "Chocolate and red velvet."

Another excited murmur floated through the crowd, this one even bigger than the first.

Maybe the baker did know her stuff.

"Yum," Susan murmured. "Can I have one of those?"

Sabrina nodded and handed over a Chocolate Ecstasy.

"I'll leave you to it then," the woman said around a mouthful. "I've got charades starting in the east wing in a few minutes."

Sabrina eyed the roomful of women quickly closing in on her. "Any men in the east wing?" She gave Susan a hopeful glance, but the woman had already started for the door.

"Only the Morgan sisters," Red chimed in as she came up to the card table where Sabrina had set up her display of goodies. "They're not actually men, but they tell everybody that they're bisexual."

"They only do that because they think it makes them more interesting to the opposite sex," Dolores chimed in, wedging in next to Red. "I'll take a red velvet. And a shirt and a mug." She pointed to the stand-up display depicting the shadow of a cowboy, hat tipped low, and the caption *Looking for a real man?* "And I'd like to fill out one of them profiles, too."

"Sure thing." Sabrina handed over the items, along with a clipboard with a questionnaire. While she'd promised Livi to turn down any more female profiles, she didn't have the heart to turn away Dolores. Or the dozen or so other women who crowded around her. Not when they looked so eager. And lonely.

Still, her real objective was to find some eligible widowers for Melba and Sarah Jean.

That, and she was doing anything and everything to keep her mind off the coming evening and the fact that she'd agreed to meet Billy at the motel at ten for night one of their agreement.

Her nipples tightened at the notion and excitement zipped up her spine. Too much excitement, considering she'd already slept with him.

But that was the point entirely.

She was going back for seconds when she never allowed herself a second rendezvous. There were no seconds when it came to her weakness. Yes, she indulged because she couldn't help the attraction, but she didn't give it a chance to morph into more.

There were no follow-up dates. No phone calls or text messages or contact of any kind. She kept it simple and brief and safe.

Until Billy.

He'd thrown a wrench into her entire system, not that she was going to let him throw her off track entirely. It was just a matter of keeping her perspective and remembering that this was a mutually beneficial arrangement.

That meant no primping for tonight or worrying over

what she was going to wear or if he was going to be on time.

She'd done all three for all of a half hour after she'd parted ways with Livi. Her partner had gone back to her room to work, while Sabrina had spent thirty minutes feeling like a virgin before her first real date. She'd finished up at the fairgrounds an hour ago with a whopping thirty cowboys to add to their database. While she still needed to scan in the profiles and send them to Kat for entry, she knew that would only take a half hour at the most.

And so she'd come here, desperate to do anything and everything to keep her mind off the coming evening and off Billy and her crazy reaction to him, and do something productive.

Yeah, right, a voice whispered as she accepted profile after profile. All the right age range, but the wrong sex.

"Is this an all-female home?" she asked after adding another profile to her growing stack. "No offense, but I was sort of hoping to find a few senior men."

"Aren't we all, sugar," said the short, round eightysomething with tight silver curls and thick glasses who reached for a mug. "Aren't we all."

SHE FINALLY FOUND a man.

Sabrina gave herself a mental high five as she rounded the corner with a few leftovers in her bakery box, headed toward the dining hall, and ran smack-dab into a silver-haired man wearing a blue polyester golf shirt and plaid walking shorts.

"Watch where you're going," he growled. "Why, you damn near ran me down."

"I'm so sorry." Sabrina grabbed the magazine he'd been carrying, which had taken a nosedive during the collision. "Let me make it up to you." She held up the box. "I've got cupcakes."

"Sarah's cupcakes?"

"You know her?"

"Who?"

"Sarah."

"She's an actual person?" He shrugged his narrow shoulders. "I just know about the cupcakes. Thought they were a brand. Like Hostess or something."

"She owns a bakery over on Main Street."

He shrugged again. "I don't get out much."

Which meant they'd never met. Which meant that maybe, just maybe, she'd hit pay dirt.

"You like red velvet?" she asked.

"You trying to send me into a diabetic coma? I don't eat sweets."

Bye-bye, Sarah.

"I like Cheetos," he went on. "Now, *there's* a snack."

Sabrina glanced around and caught a glimpse of the vending machines down the hall. "Then let me buy you a snack."

He eyed her, his pale blue eyes wary. "*You* want to buy *me* a snack? What's this?" He glanced around. "One of those hidden-camera shows or something for that there YouTube my grandson is always carrying on about?"

"No hidden camera. I just want to make up for almost running you over. That, and I'd like to tell you about my website."

"You selling something?" he asked after he let her steer him around the corner toward the vending machines.

"Not a thing." She sat her bag on one of the round tables clustered next to the machines. "Puffy or crunchy?"

"The puffy ones on account of the crunchy hurt my dentures."

She sent up a silent thank-you that Melba had agreed to be negotiable on the teeth issue.

"One bag of puffy Cheetos coming right up." She unearthed some change from her purse and fed the quarters into the machine. A few seconds later, she set the bag of chips and a Diet Fresca in front of the man.

"My name's Sabrina Collins."

"Lyle Cornflower. So if you ain't selling anything, why else would you have a website?" His expression grew serious. "You one of them bloggers?"

"No."

"Communist?"

"No."

"'Cause I know how it works. The government sends you people in to rant about all the stuff you think is wrong just to distract us from all the stuff that *is* wrong. Before you know it, the bigwigs swoop in and raise taxes and no one's the wiser."

Lyle hadn't paid taxes in a few decades, but Sabrina

didn't point that out. He was on a roll, the color in his cheeks blazing, and she couldn't help grinning.

"I can promise I'm not creating any diversions for the government."

"Why else would you have a website?"

"My business partners and I created a meet-and-greet site called FindMeACowboy.com. I wrote the business model. I'm here in town to sign up single men for the website."

"A matchmaking website?"

"Something like that. I'd like to add your profile to our growing list of men."

"I ain't no cowboy."

"Not now—" she arched an eyebrow "—but maybe once upon a time?"

"I did ride a horse once. Damn near broke my neck."

"Close enough." At least for Sarah and Melba, and that's who Sabrina was trying to match up at the moment. She pulled a pen and paper from her bag.

"You really want to find me a woman?"

"Hopefully, if your profile matches up with someone in particular. Then she can email you and you can email her, and see where it goes from there. Why, you might even have a date by next Saturday."

"For the Senior Sweetheart dance?"

"It's possible."

He shook his head. "Not no, but hell no. I already turned Melba Rose down for that and she still won't stop bugging me. You know she hates Cheetos? She even petitioned the center to take them all out of the vending machines."

"Maybe she doesn't realize they're your favorite."

"She ought to. I'm eating a bag every night when she stops by my room to see if I want to watch late-night TV with her. I say no, but she keeps coming back. She's just trying to get in my craw and catch me off guard. She has to get my signature on the petition or they won't take them out. I'm the last holdout."

Forget Melba. There was always Sarah Jean.

"Okay, we know you like Cheetos. How do you feel about cupcakes? Or pies? I'm a cream-puff girl myself."

"I'm a diabetic."

Hey, at least she'd tried.

"Say, is it seven already? My show is on." He grabbed a mug and pushed up from the table, and then he hobbled off toward the main room and the sound of CNN blazing on television.

"I say we head for the bakery and snag a cream puff." The deep voice sounded behind her and she whirled around into a rock-hard chest. Strong, familiar hands came up to steady her. Billy's husky laughter rumbled in her ears. "Easy, sugar."

"Don't do that."

"Do what?"

"Sneak up on me like that." Her gaze collided with his and her stomach bottomed out. "How long have you been standing there?"

"Long enough to know you'll do anything for a cream puff."

"I won't do anything, although I have been known to drive an extra ten minutes to indulge myself. But not very often. What are you doing here?"

"Looking for you." He glanced around. "What are you doing here?"

"I promised Sarah Jean and Melba Rose that I would find them cowboys. Melba, in particular, needs one by next Saturday night."

"And you thought Lyle Cornflower fit the bill?"

"He's the right age."

"He plays golf every Sunday with the church golf team. Cowboys don't play golf."

"So what do you want?"

"This." He leaned down and claimed her mouth for a deep, stirring kiss. "We have a deal, remember?"

"One that doesn't start for another few hours," she murmured, once she managed to drag some air into her lungs.

"I finished up early."

She braced herself against the rush of excitement and ignored the urge to touch her hair to see if everything was in place. This wasn't a date and she wasn't a virgin.

"Let's go. I thought we could get some dinner."

"I can't. I mean, you might have finished up early, but I still have a few things to do." She gathered up her purse and her bag full of leftover freebies. "I still have a few stops to make."

"Seriously?"

She nodded and then she turned on her heel and headed for the door as fast as her heels could carry her.

Because the last thing she intended to do was to have dinner with Billy Chisholm. This wasn't about dinner.

It was sex. Nothing more.

At least that's what she kept telling herself.

SHE WAS ALMOST THERE.

Sabrina clutched the edge of the sheet, her knuckles white, as she stared at the motel room ceiling a half hour later. Her nerves still buzzed. Her legs trembled. Her heart beat a frantic rhythm.

And all because of that brief, fleeting kiss at the senior center.

One measly, tired kiss.

Which meant she was even more deprived than she'd first thought.

And even more determined to work herself up so she didn't blow like Old Faithful at the first instant of contact.

She let the images from their first night together replay in her head. The impression his fingertips had made against her heated skin. The rasp of his jaw against the tenderness of her breasts. The warm press of his lips against the side of her neck. The touching...

Yes, the man had one hell of a lasting touch. That's what had her so worked up now. A kiss was just a kiss. Nothing special. Even if it had come from Billy Chisholm.

Especially because it had come from Billy Chisholm.

But the anticipation...

That she needed to get a grip on right now. Before he knocked on the door.

An orgasm. That's what she needed right now. And so she did what any healthy, red-blooded female would do. She trailed her fingers south.

Oddly enough, it didn't feel quite as good. Her hands weren't callused, her skin raspy, or her touch quite as purposeful as…

She frowned and stepped up the action, moving lower to the tender flesh between her legs. She closed her eyes and tried to picture Brad Pitt à la *World War Z*. The guy was an oldie but a goody. Unfortunately, the image just wouldn't come. Instead, she saw Billy looming over her, driving into her, and this time his moves were perfect. She came quickly, clamping down on her bottom lip to contain the scream and the screech and… *Aaah.*

Delicious sensation gripped her for a few blessed moments and she slumped back, welcoming the satisfaction sure to follow. The rush of warmth she'd felt during their night together. The punch of *oomph* that had drained the tension from her body and left her limp and lifeless and completely sated.

If only.

Instead, she still felt edgy. Nervous. Needy.

Crazy.

She ignored the strange emptiness that lingered deep inside and focused on the positive; the clenching and un-clenching between her legs, the trembling of her body, the numbness in her toes and the all-important fact that while she might still be waiting, she wasn't waiting *and* wanting.

Okay, so maybe she still wanted him, but it wasn't the all-consuming, rip-off-your-clothes-right-here-and-now want she'd felt five minutes ago.

This, she could handle.

10

SABRINA HAD BEEN naked in front of her fair share of men, but none had ever made her stomach quiver or her hands tremble the way they were right now.

It was two hours later and Billy had just shown up at her motel room. He stood just inside the doorway while she faced him and tried to remember that this was no big deal.

He was no big deal.

Her fair share, remember? She'd been there and done that, but not once had she ever felt the way she did right now with Billy Chisholm's powerful body filling up the doorway and his hot-as-a-Texas-summer gaze scorching her from her head to her toes and back up again.

He made her feel so excited and anxious and needy. No.

She didn't need Billy Chisholm, or any man like him. She simply wanted him physically. Right now. This moment.

Temporarily.

She forced her thoughts away from her fluttering stomach and shifted her attention to the six feet plus of warm male who hadn't so much as budged an inch since he'd caught sight of her.

At least his feet hadn't budged.

Her gaze lingered on the very prominent bulge beneath his jeans. Her throat went dry and she licked her lips before she could think better of it.

"Come over here and do that, sugar."

Her gaze snapped to his, to the sexy slant of his lips and the knowing light in his eyes, and she was left to wonder if she'd just imagined the flash of raw desire she'd detected when he first entered the room. A look that told her she was much more than a convenient way to spend his unchecked lust.

Right. She was as far from Billy's ideal as a woman could get, and he was far, far, far from hers. He wanted a one-night stand only.

"Well?" he drawled.

"Well, what?"

"Why don't you stop giving your bottom lip all that attention and come over here and give me some?"

"Why don't *you* come over here?"

He didn't say a word. Just stared at her with those hot eyes and that ever-widening grin, as if she'd unknowingly delivered the punch line in some private joke of his.

"What are you thinking?" she demanded before she could stop herself.

"That you're about the most stubborn woman I've ever had the misfortune to meet up with."

"I am not stubborn, and for your information, it hasn't been a picnic meeting up with you. You're stubborn yourself, and infuriating and frustrating and irritating and—"

"You look good enough to pluck from a tree and eat nice and slow." He stood barely a hand span from her. Filling up her line of vision. Drinking in all her oxygen. Zapping her common sense.

She licked her lips as her gaze riveted on his mouth. He really had a great mouth, with firm, sensual lips that made her skin itch and her insides tighten in anticipation. "It's really hot in here." She blew out a breath and fought for another. "Can we just get to it?"

He stared at her long and hard, his grin faltering for a quick second when his gaze dropped to drink in the rapid rise and fall of her chest. *"Hurry up and get to it?"* He reached out and caught a drop of perspiration as it slid down the valley between her breasts. His touch lingered and her heart thudded a frantic rhythm against his fingertip. "We'll get to it, darlin', but there won't be anything hurried about it."

And then his mouth touched hers.

Sabrina Collins had the sassiest mouth Billy Chisholm had ever heard on a woman, all right. And the sweetest he'd ever tasted. Her lips parted at the first moment of contact, and for several heartbeats Billy actually forgot that he liked his kisses slow and teasing.

There was nothing slow about the way he stroked his

tongue along the length of hers and plunged deep into her mouth. Nothing teasing about the purposeful way he ate at her lips, as if she were his only sustenance and he'd gone far too long without.

He had.

That was the only thought that drew him back to reality and helped him resist the sudden urge to bend her over in that next instant and sink as deep as possible into her soft, warm body, until he forgot where he ended and she began. Until he forgot everything—the upcoming ride and the pressure to step up and take his brother's place—everything, save the woman in his arms and the need heating his blood.

Slow and easy.

He gathered his control and fought for a leisurely pace because as much as he wanted Sabrina Collins, he wanted that PBR buckle, and that meant getting a good workout right now.

The kiss softened as he suckled her bottom lip and wrung a frustrated moan from her.

He slid his hands up her arms, over her shoulders, learning her shape, the dips and curves near her collarbone, the soft, satiny slopes of her breasts.

He lifted her onto the desk, parted her long legs and stepped between her thighs. Her heat cradled the rock-hard erection pulsing beneath his jeans. He thumbed her nipples and caught her cry of pleasure with his mouth, the sound exciting him almost as much as the knowledge that he was finally going to slake the lust that woke him every morning, his body taut and throbbing after a restless night spent dreaming and wanting.

He gave up her lips after a deep, delicious kiss to nibble down her chin, the underside of her jaw. He licked a fiery path to the beat of her pulse, and teased and nibbled at the hollow of her throat until she gasped. Then he moved on, inhaling her sweet, fragrant smell, savoring the flavor of her skin. An echoing flame leaped through him, burning hotter, brighter...

Easy.

He leaned back long enough to drink in the sight of her, her head thrown back, her eyes closed, her breasts arched in silent invitation. Dipping his head, he took a slow, leisurely lap at her nipple. The tip quivered, expanded, reached out and begged for more. He licked her again, slow and easy and thorough, before drawing the flesh deep into his mouth and sucking long and hard. A moan vibrated up her throat and she gasped, grasping at his shoulders.

The grasping he could handle. It was the way she wrapped her legs around his waist and rubbed herself up against his aching length that scattered his common sense. He felt her heat through the tight denim. Anticipated it.

Her desperate fingers worked the button of his jeans, then the zipper. It stuck for a heart-pounding moment, the teeth stretched too tight over his straining length. A swift yank, a frenzied *zippp* and he could breathe again.

One silky fingertip touched the swollen head of his

erection peeking up at the waistband of his underwear, and the air lodged in his throat. So much for breathing.

He caught her head in his hands, his fingers splaying in her hair, anchoring her for the long, deep probe of his tongue.

"Billy!" A knock on the door punctuated the shout, the noise piercing the passionate fog Billy found himself lost in. He stiffened, breaking the kiss to gasp for air as footsteps sounded on the walkway outside.

Sabrina's forehead furrowed and her eyelids fluttered open. "What's wrong?"

Before Billy could answer, he heard Cole's voice again on the other side of the motel room door. "Hey, Billy! You in there? Listen, I was minding my own business at the rodeo arena when I ran into that reporter Curt Calhoun. You know, the one who did the follow-up episode on *Famous Texas Outlaws*. Seems he's still poking around. I gave him a statement, but he said he wants to talk to you. Billy? I know you're here, bud. Your truck's in the parking lot." The words trailed off as the knob twisted, the door creaked.

Billy fought with his zipper, but he didn't have enough time. The best he could do in the name of decency was yank his T-shirt down over his open fly as he whirled, Sabrina's nude body hidden behind him.

"There's a shitload of reporters waiting to get a statement from the bull riders and—" The words stumbled to a halt as Cole's gaze hooked on the bare knee peeking past Billy's jean-clad thigh. He looked puzzled for an eighth of a second, before a knowing light gleamed in his violet eyes. "Sorry, man. I—I didn't know you had company."

Billy tried to ignore the soft hands resting against his shoulder blades, the warm breath rushing against the back of his neck. "They want an interview now?"

"Who?" Cole shook his head as if to clear the cobwebs. "The reporters? Yeah. There're three in the motel lobby, not counting Calhoun who's on his way right now. I told 'em you'd be along any second, but I'll just let them know the timing is bad. Maybe they can catch you tomorrow." Just before the door clicked shut, Cole said, "You just go back to what you were doing and I'll get rid of them."

The best advice Billy had heard in a helluva long time. That's what his throbbing body said, but his conscience, his damn conscience, kept him from turning and taking Sabrina in his arms.

"Who is Curt Calhoun?" she asked quietly as he fought for a deep, calming breath.

"A reporter. *The* reporter who put together the *Famous Texas Outlaws* episode that features my dad."

"Your dad?"

He expected a lot of things from Sabrina, namely the slide of her arms, the touch of her fingertips, a whispered "Let them wait." She wasn't a woman to take no for an answer when she wanted something and she obviously wanted him. But he didn't expect her to pull away from him.

"Maybe you ought to go see what they want." Her

hands grasped the gaping edges of his jeans. Soft fingertips grazed his erection as she slid the button into place and tugged at his zipper.

His hands closed over hers, helping her until the teeth closed and he was rock-hard and throbbing beneath the denim once again. As if the action had tried her patience as much as his, he heard the deep draw of her breath. Relief.

"You go on," she told him. "I'll wait here."

Billy wasn't about to argue. He started walking, conscious of her eyes on him and even more aware of the need gripping his insides. It would be so easy to turn back to her, to forget about Curt Calhoun the other reporters who would guarantee him top-notch media coverage for the upcoming rodeo.

Too easy.

He kept walking.

Besides, as eager as he was right now, he wouldn't last a decent minute. Sabrina would be flat on her back and he'd be inside her for less than a heartbeat, and Billy didn't want that. He liked his loving long and slow and fierce. He'd never had much of a fondness for quickies. He abstained for months on end when he was in training, and so when he indulged, he liked to make the most of his time. To commit every breathless sigh, every soft moan to memory.

He liked things slow and he wasn't about to change his mind on account of a bad case of lust.

Not now. Not ever.

His dad was Silas Chisholm. *The* Silas Chisholm.

The truth crystallized as Billy's words echoed in Sabrina's ears.

He wasn't just Billy Chisholm the up-and-coming bull rider. He was one of Silas Chisholm's three sons. Her heart pounded in her chest at the realization because Silas had been one of the biggest stories to ever come out of a small town.

A career-making story.

If she could find a fresh angle, that is.

She wasn't sure if there was one, but it warranted some serious thought and so she'd let Billy walk away when the only thing she'd really wanted to do was haul him close, to hell with any reporter.

She'd run across Curt Calhoun's name in connection with Silas when she'd started her research last night. Calhoun had hosted the original *Famous Texas Outlaws* story, as well as the recent "Where Are They Now?" episode that had aired only a week or so ago. But he hadn't packed up and shipped out after the episode.

No, he was still here. Still digging.

Because there was more information still to come to light?

Maybe, and it was that maybe that sent a burst of excitement through Sabrina and had her scrambling to right her clothes after Billy disappeared.

A few tugs and she headed straight for her computer. Opening a document file, she started brainstorming a list of questions that she meant to ask Billy. Tactfully, of course. She'd seen his reaction tonight and so she had no doubt that he wouldn't be too keen on her fishing for information, let alone writing a story about his past.

If there was a story.

The doubt echoed and she considered the possibility that maybe it was over and done with. Maybe Curt Calhoun was hanging around for a different reason altogether, a new story that had nothing to do with the late Silas Chisholm, or maybe he had new suspicions that were just plain false.

There was only one way to find out.

She was going to keep her eyes and ears open, and dig for information whenever she had the chance. That, and she couldn't shake the niggle in her gut that told her something was up.

More than just Billy's libido.

Particularly when he didn't head back to her room when he finished up with the reporters.

Instead, she heard the grumble of his truck and the spew of gravel as he pulled out of the parking lot and disappeared for the rest of the evening.

Even more than suspicion, disappointment ricocheted through her and she resigned herself to the possibility that he'd changed his mind.

Hours passed before he finally proved her wrong and knocked on her door just this side of midnight.

"What took you so long?" she asked, her heart racing and her body trembling. From excitement and anticipation and relief. Both heightened because Billy wasn't just a way to break her dry spell. He was her ticket to a real story.

No way was she so worked up because she'd thought for those few hours that he truly had changed his mind, and she'd been nervous. No. *Way.*

"I had some business to take care of with my brothers." He arched his back as if his muscles ached and exhaustion tugged at him.

She lifted an eyebrow. "What kind of business?"

"A favor for Jesse. He's got this cockamamy idea…" His words trailed off and he shook his head, as if he'd said more than he wanted to. As if he'd wanted to say more. "It doesn't matter now." He wiped a hand over his face before his attention shifted to her and a hungry light fueled his eyes. "What do you say we get out of here?"

"But I thought we were going to do it—"

"We are," he cut in, closing the distance between them, his lips finding hers. "But not here. I don't want to risk another distraction."

Neither did she. She wanted him all to herself.

For sex, that is. And information. And that was it.

At least that's what she was telling herself.

She nodded, and then she grabbed her purse and followed him out to his pickup truck.

11

BILLY MEANT TO get busy at the motel.

At least that was the idea that had been cooking in his head since they'd first agreed to get together again. A nice, neutral room at the local motel just like the one they'd used during their first encounter.

But then Cole had shown up. And a bunch of reporters. And he'd found himself stuck in the lobby for way too long since Curt Calhoun had insisted on walking down memory lane and bugging him about his dad.

No comment.

That was his standard response. While Billy had no problem talking about the past, he didn't want to give the media any more fuel for gossip than they already had. And for whatever reason, Curt Calhoun had a bug up his butt.

The man should have left last week like all the others who'd gathered in Lost Gun for the "Where Are They Now?" episode. Instead, he was hanging around, asking more questions, as if he knew that something was up.

As if he knew about the money.

Like hell.

Nobody knew except Billy and his brothers, and Big Earl and his great granddaughter, Casey. And Big Earl surely wasn't talking. He could barely remember his name half the time now. And Casey? She wasn't the social type. Even more, Jesse had promised her a sizable reward if she helped them uncover the money while keeping her mouth shut.

Billy pushed the thoughts out of his head and concentrated on the task at hand—finding some much-needed privacy with Sabrina.

He was too preoccupied. Too uptight. Too damn tired.

He needed some sleep.

But first he needed her.

Now.

So he'd opted for the quickest solution instead of hauling butt all the way out to the interstate and over to the next county. He'd turned off the main road and driven here.

For convenience' sake, of course.

It wasn't because he wanted her to see his cabin, to actually like it. And no way was it because he'd been fantasizing about seeing her in his bed for the past few days. And nights. And every moment in between.

This, he told himself again as he stared at the newly built cabin visible just beyond the break between two towering Texas pines, was nothing more than pure convenience.

"This isn't a motel," she said, her gaze following his.

"What was your first clue?" Billy killed the engine and climbed from the front seat.

"All right, smart-ass." Her voice followed him and he grinned.

"It's not much," he said as he rounded the front and reached her door. "Just something I've been building in my spare time." He helped her from the passenger seat and started walking toward the cabin. "It's still a work in progress, but the walls are up and it has all the bare necessities to get us through the night. Lights and running water and a shower and even a working kitchen—"

"It's really big." Her voice carried after him as she followed him down the path.

"—and the toilet is fully functional—"

"And isolated."

"—and there's a king-size bed with fresh sheets and—"

"And really beautiful."

"—and there's a fireplace in the living room, not that we want a fire this time of year, but— What did you just say?" He stopped and turned on her so fast she bumped into his chest.

"I said it's beautiful." She touched one of the hand-carved beams, and her gaze met his. "It's amazing that you actually did all of this yourself. You did great work."

A strange warmth spread through him, a feeling he quickly pushed back down as his gaze dropped to her shoes.

Her attention followed his and she picked up her feet,

dislodging one of her three-inch stilettos, which had sunk in the soft ground. "Beautiful, but muddy."

"We could drive back into town if it's too rustic for you. Not that the motel is all that much better, but at least there are people around. The Dairy Freeze is nearby."

She cast a glance past him and something strangely close to fear flashed in her eyes before fading into hard, glittering determination. She planted her hands on her hips. "I'm not interested in an ice cream."

His eyes glittered. "Is that so?"

"You bet your cowboy hat. We made a deal and it's time we get started."

Before he could so much as blink, her free hand reached out and gripped his collar. And she hauled him close for a spectacular kiss that overshadowed anyone and everyone in Billy's past. He forgot every woman, every encounter, *everything* except Sabrina and what she was doing to him with her lips.

SEX, THAT'S ALL THIS WAS, Sabrina told herself, throwing herself into the single act of kissing Billy Chisholm, desperate to ignore the strange feelings that had assailed her the moment they'd rolled to a stop in front of the cabin—the sprawling, still-under-construction cabin with the hand-carved porch swing hanging out front and a dusty old saddle draped over the porch railing and several old fashioned milk cans overflowing with sunflowers. One look at the swing and she'd had the sudden vision of herself, barefoot and pregnant, rocking back and forth, a sunflower stuffed behind one ear, Billy planted next to her—

No.

No, no, no, no, *no.*

Not the barefoot and pregnant part. It was the man himself she was objecting to. The wrong man. A cowboy.

The cowboy.

Fat chance.

She'd vowed off cowboys a long time ago when she'd watched her mother wait up for her father night after night. She'd loved him so much and he'd used that emotion against her. No matter how much he'd cheated on her, he'd always managed to sweet-talk his way back into her good graces. He'd smiled and teased and charmed and made promises he'd had no intention of keeping, and *bam,* everything had been perfect. Until the next night when he headed back out to the honky-tonk and started carousing all over again.

He'd used her mother. Worse, the woman had let him. She'd known what he was up to. The whole town had. Still, she'd let him get away with it because she'd been powerless to stop it. Weak. Spineless.

Then and now.

Her mother was back at it with yet another cowboy, letting him use her because she feared letting go of the ideal that she'd built up in her head. She feared losing her *real* cowboy for good.

Not Sabrina.

She was working Billy Chisholm out of her system

and killing the whole cowboy ideal right here and now. And she was not—repeat, was not—falling for him the way her mother had fallen for her father, no matter how many porch swings he had hanging outside his cabin. Or how many sunflowers—her favorite flower as a matter of fact—he stuffed into those milk cans. Or how good he kissed. Or how he pulled her close and rubbed the base of her spine with his thumb until she wanted to purr. Or how he held her close, his arms solid and strong and possessive, as if she actually meant more to him than a few moments of pleasure.

This wasn't about forever. It was about this moment, this kiss, *this*…

For the next few moments, she drank in the taste and feel of him, ran her hands up and down his solid arms, relished the ripple of muscle as he cupped her buttocks and pulled her closer.

He rocked her, his hardness pressing into her and heat flowered low in her belly, spreading from one nerve ending to the next until every inch of her body burned.

She moaned into his mouth and, without breaking the kiss, he swung her into his arms and headed for the cabin.

A few seconds later, her feet touched down in the bedroom. The walls were still raw and unfinished, just bare frame filled with insulation, except for one. Floor-length windows spanned from corner to corner, overlooking the surrounding forest and a small creek that shimmered in the distance. A king-size bed, piled neatly with colorful quilts, sat in the middle of the room, looking out of place amid the surrounding chaos of wood and tools. Beams crisscrossed the ceiling, framing a tarp-covered soon-to-be skylight. Sawdust covered the floors, and as much as Sabrina liked the soft floral scent of her potpourri-scented bedroom back in L.A., she found herself inhaling, filling her lungs with the sharp aroma of fresh air and Texas pine and Billy.

She pressed herself up against him again, the need building until she clawed at his shirt. He caught her wrists and pulled back, his grin slow and wicked and dangerous.

"Easy. We've got all night, sugar."

"We've got a few hours," she said as she unfastened her skirt and let the material pool at her ankles. "I have to put in an appearance at the dance tonight, so you'd better start undressing."

"If you want to dance, sugar, I can accommodate you right here." His bright, heated gaze slid from hers to roam down her body—her parted lips and heaving chest and quivering thighs—and back up again.

"I'm not going there to dance. I'm going to work. I need more men."

"Not tonight you don't. Tonight all you need is me. Us." The hands that slid from her shoulder to her collarbone, and down, were strong and sure and possessive.

As if he was branding her his and only his.

Just as the thought struck, he touched the tip of her nipple through the thin fabric of her blouse. The ripe tip throbbed in response and she barely caught the whimper that jumped to her lips.

He pressed a kiss to her lips then, coaxing them open with his tongue before delving deep for a long, heart-pounding moment. "Don't hold back," he murmured when he finally pulled away. "I like to hear you."

He parted her blouse and touched her, his hot fingertips tracing the edge of her bra where lace met skin, and she forgot everything except the need churning inside her.

Sabrina closed her eyes and tilted her head back, arching her chest forward. Strong fingers stroked her nipples through the lace for several long moments until she gasped.

A deep male chuckle warmed her skin a heartbeat before his hot mouth touched her neck, licking and nibbling as his hands worked at her bra clasp. A few tugs and the lace cups fell away.

She all but screamed at the first stroke of his callused thumb over her bare breast. The next several moments passed in a dizzying blur as he plucked and rolled her sensitive nipples, until they were red and ripe and aching for more.

His hands slid down her rib cage and warmed her stomach. A deep male growl vibrated up his throat when his hands slid into her panties and found her wet and ready. One fingertip parted her swollen flesh and dipped inside.

She cried out, grabbing his shoulders, clutching fabric as she fought to feel his bare skin against her own.

He leaned back far enough and let her pull the material up and over his head. She tossed the T-shirt and went for his jeans, but he'd beaten her to the punch, his tanned fingers working at the zipper.

Metal grated and the jeans sagged onto his hips. He stepped back far enough to push them down and kick them free until he stood before her wearing only a pair of black boxer briefs. He was rock hard beneath the clingy black cotton. A heartbeat later, the full length of him sprang forward, huge and greedy, as he pushed his underwear down and kicked it to the side.

But it wasn't the sight of him naked and tanned and fully aroused that took her breath away, it was the heat burning in his gaze, making his eyes a bright, mesmerizing violet.

Her hands went to her open blouse, but he pushed her fingers aside to peel the shirt and bra away from her flushed skin.

"Aren't you forgetting something?" she breathed when he made no move to remove her last item of clothing—a pair of slinky bikini panties cut high on the thighs.

"Soon," he murmured. He cupped her, his palm warm through the thin covering.

An ache flowered low in her belly. "Soon isn't soon enough. I want to feel you. Now." Anxiety zipped up and down her spine, along with a ripple of unmistakable fear.

Because she didn't *want* to want him so deeply. So desperately. Billy Chisholm was a cowboy.

If only that thought didn't turn her on even more.

12

HE DIPPED ONE finger past the elastic, into the steamy heat between her legs. He stroked and teased and a sweet pressure tightened low in her belly.

"Then it's settled. You're not working tonight." For emphasis, he slid his finger into her slowly, tantalizingly, stirring every nerve to vibrant awareness until he was as deep as he could go, and then he withdrew at the same leisurely pace.

Advance, retreat, until her heart pounded so hard and her breath came so fast, she thought she would hyperventilate.

She was close.

So close…

"Not yet," he murmured, withdrawing his hand before dropping to his knees in front of her.

He touched his mouth to her navel, dipped his tongue inside and slid his hands around to cup her bottom for a long moment before moving his mouth lower. His tongue dipped under the waistband of her panties. He licked her bare flesh before drawing back to drag his mouth over her lace-covered mound. His lips feathered a kiss over her sensitive skin, and her legs buckled. Her hands went to his bare shoulders to keep her from falling.

A warm chuckle sent shivers down the inside of her thighs before he lifted his head and caught the waistband of her underwear with his teeth. He drew the material down, lips and teeth skimming her bare flesh in a delicious friction that made her want to scream. Her entire body trembled by the time she stepped free.

"My turn."

"I don't have any underwear on." He pushed to his feet and faced her.

"I'll improvise." She knelt and kissed his navel, swirling her tongue and relishing the deep male groan that vibrated the air around them. She grasped him in her hand, running her palm down the length of his erection. He was hot and hard and she did what she'd been wanting to do ever since she'd seen him standing there completely nude. She took him into her mouth and laved him with her tongue as a low hiss issued from between his lips.

He grasped her head, his fingers splaying in her hair, guiding her, urging her—

"Stop." The word was little more than a groan before he pulled her to her feet and tumbled her down onto the bed.

She watched as he withdrew a foil packet from his jeans pocket and put on a condom in record time.

"I thought you wanted slow and easy," she said as he settled himself between her thighs, his penis pressing into her a decadent inch.

"It'll be easy," he promised. "I'm just not so sure about the *slow* part." Before she could comment, he pressed her thighs wider, grasped her hips and slid into her with one deep thrust.

He stilled for a long moment, letting her feel every pulsing vibrating inch of him as he filled her completely.

She closed her eyes, fighting back the sudden tears that threatened to overwhelm her. This was crazy. This was all about feeling good, not about *feeling*.

That was a lesson her mother had never been able to learn. That sex wasn't love and that a man good with his body wasn't necessarily as skilled with his heart.

"Are you okay?" His voice was soft and deep and so tender she had to fight back another wave of tears.

Tears, of all the silly, ridiculous, *emotional* things....

She swallowed and forced her voice past the lump in her throat. "Stop talking and just ride, cowboy. Just ride."

His mouth opened and she thought he was going to make a smart comeback, but then he dipped his head and his lips closed over her nipple. Thankfully. She needed a distraction from the strange feelings threatening to overwhelm her.

All thought faded into a wave of delicious pressure as he suckled her long and hard, his erection pulsing inside her. The sensation of him drawing on her breast and her body drawing on his was a double whammy. Twice as delicious. As distracting.

He moved, pumping into her, pushing her higher— stroke after stroke—until she cried out, her nails digging into his back as she climaxed.

Several frantic heartbeats later, her eyelids fluttered open just in time to see him throw his head back, his eyes clamped tightly shut. He thrust deep one final time and stiffened, every muscle in his body going rigid. Her name tumbled from his lips, riding a raw moan of pure male satisfaction.

He collapsed beside her and gathered her close, pulling her back against him in spoon fashion. His chest was solid against her back, his arms strong and powerful around her. Warmth seeped through her, lulling her heartbeat for the next several minutes as their bodies cooled.

Her gaze went to the floor-length windows and the sparkling lake just beyond. The light of the full moon danced across the shimmering surface.

"Wow," she breathed, the word so soft and hushed she marveled when she heard his deep voice in response.

"You should see it late at night when the moon is full."

"How did you ever find this place?"

"My oldest brother, Jesse, found it a long time ago. He was hiking up here in the woods one time and stumbled on this old, abandoned hunting shack. It wasn't much. Just a tin roof and four walls, but it was quiet and calm. We used to come up here to get away from our father whenever he drank too much." His gaze brightened for a split second. "We spent way too much time here."

"So your dad was an alcoholic?"

"That was his second calling. He was a criminal first and foremost. He robbed one of the local banks."

"Your dad is Silas Chisholm," she murmured, her heart pounding in her chest at the mention of the man. This was it. Her chance to ask him about his past. About that night.

"What about your mom?" she voiced one of the dozens of questions now running through her brain. Not nearly the most provocative, but then she was trying to play it smart and slow. If she started drilling him, he would more than likely freeze up or tell her to take a hike. Neither possibility was one she wanted to risk. "Where was she during that time?"

"She took off when I was a few months old. She died a few years later in a car wreck." He shrugged. "I didn't really know her. What about you? Where are your parents?"

Divert and keep prodding. That's what her head said. Ask him another question. Get him talking more.

At the same time, she didn't miss the curiosity in his gaze, the interest, as if her reply truly mattered to him. "I just have my mom," she heard herself say. "She lives in a little town about a half hour outside of Houston. My dad wasn't the faithful type. He'd cheat. My mom would kick him out. Then she'd take him back. Then it would start all over again. About ten years ago, he cheated again, but my mom didn't have the chance to take him back. He walked out for good and never came back." She expected the mention of her father to stir the usual anger and fear and loneliness, but with Billy's arms around her and his lips so close to her ear, she didn't feel the same twist of hurt. She felt warm and wanted and content, and she realized in a startling instant that she liked having Billy curled around her as much as she'd liked having him deep inside.

Maybe more.

"I really need to get dressed," she blurted, desperate for a quick exit strategy from the crazy feelings and the all-important fact that for those few seconds as she'd talked about her father, she'd forgotten all about her story.

Before she could blink, she found herself flipped onto her back. Billy glared down at her for a long moment as if the comment actually bothered him. Ridiculous, of course, because nothing she said or did seemed to really shake that charming, controlled demeanor.

Until now.

His expression eased, quickly killing her theory as a slow, sensual smile crept across his lips.

"Nah, sugar. That," he said, pausing to kiss her Hello Kitty tattoo and one pert nipple, "was just the warm-up." He slid down her body, his large hands going to the inside of her thighs. He spread her legs wide and scorched her with a heated glance before reaching for the ice-cold beer sitting on the nightstand. Popping the top, he took a long swig before dribbling just a hint into her belly button.

The cold liquid tickled its way across her skin and she shivered. But not from the temperature. From the determined look in his eyes.

"The main event starts now." And then he dipped his head and lapped at the golden liquid with his tongue, providing a much-needed diversion from the tender feelings coiling inside her.

She didn't want tender. She wanted wild and wicked and hot, and over. That's what she really wanted. To be done with him. To move on.

Physically that is.

The trouble was, she wasn't done with him. Not yet, anyhow.

Not. Just. Yet.

13

SHE WAS NOT going to watch.

That's what Sabrina told herself as she drove back to the motel after yet another exhausting day at the rodeo arena.

So what if it was Saturday? The day of the semifinals? The ride that would dictate whether he went to the next level?

Whether *they* went to the next level and continued with one more week of their arrangement, or called it quits tonight.

She stifled the anxiety that rolled through her. If it ended, it ended. All the better. She was already having enough trouble getting herself out and about before he opened his eyes. Sleeping in would be a good thing. Welcome.

No, she wasn't watching.

Not only couldn't she care less if tonight ended their temporary arrangement, but she certainly didn't want to see him in his element. It was one thing to know she was sleeping with a bona fide cowboy and quite another to see the proof for herself.

At least when he touched her in the dead of night she could pretend that he was as far from her Not Happening list as a man could get. She could even picture him in a three-piece suit or a policeman's uniform or something equally acceptable. In the dead of night, he could be any man.

But seeing him thrashing about on a thousand-pound bull would only confirm what she already knew deep in her gut.

No, she wasn't watching.

She scanned in the profiles she'd collected that day and emailed them to Kat for entry into the database. She did some online research on Silas Chisholm and the bank robbery. Oddly enough, the research didn't stir the usual ideas when it came to a story. The more she discovered, the more she thought about Billy. But not about his childhood or the crime or a great angle to pursue for the story. Instead, she found herself thinking about the man he'd become. A man so different from his sorry excuse for a parent. Billy was kind and brave and honest and—

Ugh, she needed to think about something else. Anything else.

She gave up the research and turned her attention to Sarah. She and Livi were making slow and steady progress signing up cowboys, and while she knew she should devote her time and energy to that, she couldn't stop thinking about the bakery owner. The woman was

lonely. Sabrina had seen it in her eyes. The same loneliness she'd seen in her own mother's eyes every time
Sabrina's father had walked out the door, which was
why she'd agreed to help the woman in the first place.
And so she spent the next few hours going over various
date possibilities, including Harwin who called bingo
at the VFW hall. While he ran his own plumbing company and spent most of his time in overalls and tennis shoes, he had been voted Hottest Bachelor Over
Forty at last year's Fourth of July picnic, which earned
him a personal evaluation. While he wasn't much in
the looks department, he'd earned the title—which had
been voted on by the single members of the ladies' aux-
iliary—somehow.

Maybe he was the legendary lover Sarah was looking for.

She eyed the photo she'd found on Google depicting
him midcall at last week's bingo night. Receding hair-
line. Beady eyes. Double chin.

Maybe not.

Still, she had to see for herself.

Her mind made up, she went back to doing anything—everything—except turning on the TV. She took
a shower. She painted her nails. She painted her toenails.
She ate three Reese's peanut butter cups *and* a Snickers.

Okay, so maybe she'd watch for just a few minutes.

The thought struck as she swallowed the last bite of
peanut butter and chocolate. She should have known
nothing good ever came from a triple dose of chocolate,
but desperate times, as the saying went.

The ancient TV fired to life, the screen rolling and pitching as Sabrina flipped through the channels. She hit the local station and *bam,* the rodeo arena filled the screen. Thousands of screaming fans loaded the stands and in the center a bull kicked and pitched, desperately trying to throw cowboy number 13.

Her gaze went to the leaderboard in the background and Billy's name, which sat next to the number 22. Each cowboy went three rounds, then the scores were added together and averaged for a final tally. Her gaze drank in the two scores posted. He still had number three to go.

Three more cowboys—all of whom hit the dust before the buzzer sounded—and Billy was up.

Sabrina perched on the edge of the bed, her heart in her throat as she watched the chute open. The bull pitched forward, but Billy held on tight.

One thousand one.

Another vicious twist and he jerked to the right.

One thousand two. One thousand three.

The bull reared up and Billy leaned forward.

One thousand four. One thousand five.

Another twist and Billy went to the side.

And then the damnable TV flickered and the screen went blank.

"ARE YOU OKAY?" Sabrina demanded the second she hauled open the door to her motel room.

It was one in the morning and Billy hadn't even had a chance to knock. She'd obviously been waiting for him.

Worried about him.

A burst of warmth went through him and he barely ignored the urge to haul her into his arms and bury his face in her sweet-smelling neck. But hugging for the sheer closeness wasn't part of their arrangement. That, and his shoulder hurt like a son of a bitch, despite a triple dose of ibuprofen the rodeo doc had given him and two hours spent in the training room with an extra-large ice pack.

"Hello to you, too." He moved past her into the small motel room and tossed his hat onto the dresser. "I'm a little bruised up but I'm okay." He couldn't help his grin as reality hit him. "You watched me ride."

"Not on purpose." She shrugged as if trying to dismiss the truth. "I was looking for *Cupcake Wars* and there you were." Her gaze met his and he saw the worry swimming deep. "But then the TV messed up before your last ride ended. I saw you go to the side and then the screen went black." Concern fueled her voice. "What happened? Did he throw you?"

"Damn straight he did." He sank onto the edge of the bed. "But I managed to hang on anyway."

"That's great."

"Not so great. Hanging on sideways doesn't exactly command a high score. I lost major points for losing my seat, but I still hit the buzzer."

"And?"

A grin pulled at the corner of his mouth. "And I made the finals."

"That's great!" She smiled, and damned if the sight didn't make him forget the pain in his shoulder for those next few moments as the realization of what that meant sizzled in the air between them. "I mean, um, that's great for you," she rushed on when his own grin widened. "You're one step closer to your dream."

"Damn straight." He leaned down to pull off his boots, and his shoulder cried with the motion. He winced and caught his breath.

She was beside him in that next instant. "What's wrong?"

"Damn bull pulled my shoulder out of socket." He noted the sudden brightness of her gaze and something softened inside him. "But I'm fine now. Sore, but everything's back where it needs to be."

"Maybe you ought to soak in the tub, or at least climb into a hot shower."

He shook his head. "I already had a shower. All I really want to do now is get into bed."

She nodded and helped him pull off his boots. A few seconds later, his clothes lay in a heap next to the bed. He crawled between the sheets and sank into one fluffy pillow while she shed her clothes and crawled into bed next to him.

She looked so soft with her hair mussed and her face free of most of the makeup she usually wore, and something tightened in his chest.

She wasn't the most beautiful woman he'd ever been with. Logically, he knew that. But damned if he could recall even one that was sweeter or more perfect than the woman next to him.

The realization sent a wave of panic through him and

he kissed her roughly on her full lips and rolled over, putting his back to her before he gave in to the urge to lose himself in her tight, hot body.

"What are you doing?"

"Going to sleep," he grumbled into the pillow.

"But you can't sleep. I mean, I know you had a close call and all, but you're okay. You are okay, right? That bull didn't stomp any important parts, did he?"

He couldn't help the smile that tugged at his lips. "Nothing below the waist, if that's what you're worried about. I'm just exhausted."

And scared shitless because not once had Billy been so focused on any one woman. Ever.

And not just for the past few seconds.

Her image had haunted him all evening while he'd walked the rodeo arena and watched the other contestants. When he'd climbed onto the bull for a ride that would make or break his career. When he'd hit the dust after hanging on for dear life. Especially when he'd hit the dust.

For a few seconds as the pain had gripped his body, he'd thought that maybe that was it. That he was biting the dust once and for all. And instead of thinking what a damn shame it would be because he was this close to nabbing his own championship, he'd thought of her.

Her sweet face. Her sexy body. *Her.*

Not that it would last.

Billy had been there and done that, and while it felt really good right now, he knew it would end. It always ended.

Better to put a little distance between them until his head was screwed on straight again. The fall he'd taken after the buzzer. That's what had knocked his senses loose. That was why he was thinking such foolish thoughts, like how he wanted to curl up next to her and nuzzle her neck even more than he wanted to slide into her hot, tight body.

Holy crap, that bull really had jarred something loose upstairs.

That, and he really *was* tired. Every bone in his body hurt. His head throbbed. No wonder he wasn't thinking straight.

"Sweet dreams," he murmured.

"Maybe for you," she grumbled as she rolled the other way.

Billy closed his eyes and drew in a deep breath, the effort stirring a sharp pain, thanks to his bruised ribs. He sucked in another deep breath and bit back a groan.

She didn't move for a long moment, but then the mattress dipped as she turned over and scooted up next to him.

In the back of his mind, an alarm bell went off, but the pain was still needling him and so he didn't heed the warning. He felt the soft press of her lips on his temple and his heart stopped for a long moment. The familiar scent of warm woman and fresh peaches filled his nostrils and soothed the throbbing at his temples. Her arm slid around him and her fingers lightly stroked his rib cage, and it was the last thing he remembered before falling asleep.

14

WITH EACH DAY that passed, Billy was finding it harder and harder to remember that this was just sex. Temporary.

Because it felt more permanent than anything else in his life. More right. He found himself looking forward to the little things. Counting on them. Seeing her smile when he kissed the tip of her nose. Holding her until the crack of dawn. Listening to her off-key singing in the shower. *Liking* her off-key singing in the shower.

Sabrina Collins was the last woman he needed to fall into like with. She was out of here in less than four days. She'd made no false promises, left no room for maybe.

Soon their arrangement would be over and she would be long gone, and Billy could get back to his career and finishing up the additions to his cabin and the stuff that really mattered.

Not the crazy feelings pushing and pulling inside him. It was time to switch those off and simply enjoy his last few nights with her.

At the same time, he couldn't help wanting her to feel the same way. To miss him when he climbed out of bed in the morning, to look forward to his company every night, to want to see him in a capacity that didn't involve getting naked.

Hell, maybe she already did.

The thing was, there was no way to really know because the sex was muddying the waters. She might already like the little things as much as he did. She might like him.

Enough to stay?

He wasn't sure, but there was only one way to find out.

"What is all this?" Sabrina stood at the island stove, in the middle of Billy's newly renovated kitchen, surrounded by pots and pans and black granite countertops cluttered with all the ingredients for Billy's infamous Hell, Fire & Brimstone Chili.

"I make it for the cowboys every year before the finals. I competed once in the actual cook-off when I was sixteen—Eli made me since I was too young to ride and he was trying to get me more involved at the arena—and it was such a huge hit that I still cook up a mess every year and drop it off at the rodeo grounds for the workers. It's my own recipe," he'd told her earlier that afternoon when he'd stopped by her booth at the festival to tell her they would have to postpone tonight's rendezvous. He had too much to do to get enough chili ready for thirty rodeo hands by tomorrow morning. All night. That's what he'd said.

Unless she wanted to help him. They could get it done in half the time and get on with the sex.

And so she was here, smack-dab in the middle of her worst domestic nightmare, because Sabrina had never been much of a cook. She'd never wanted to be after watching her mother slave away for her father, who'd never appreciated it.

But this wasn't cooking for the sake of pleasing some ungrateful cowboy. This was just part of her arrangement with Billy.

At least that's what she told herself as she moved about his kitchen while he stood at a nearby countertop and seasoned a mountain of ground beef. He'd pulled his shirt tails free of his jeans and unfastened the top buttons of his Western shirt. The vee afforded her a glimpse of silky chest hair and tanned skin.

Her stomach tingled and her nipples tightened and all was right with her world.

Sex.

That's all it was between them. It wasn't as if she liked standing next to him, working side by side, as a slow, twangy country song drifted from a nearby radio. It was all about the heat that raged between them. The intense lust. The overwhelming physical attraction.

She held tight to the thought as she rinsed the uncooked pinto beans and dumped them in a large pot. Thankfully, she could feel his eyes following her as she filled the pot with water and left the beans soaking, to turn her attention to the stove. Her skin prickled with awareness as he moved next to her and fed the seasoned meat into another pot before kicking up the heat. Her nipples tingled. Her tummy quivered.

He turned and his arm brushed against her breast. A tiny thrill of excitement zipped up her spine. He stared deep into her eyes and for a split second, she felt him lean forward. His warm breath brushed her lips and she closed her eyes. This was more like it. They could forget all this domestic crap and get to the really good stuff. He was going to kiss her—

"I've got a few more pots in the car," he murmured before planting a kiss on the tip of her nose. "Hold down the fort. I'll be right back."

Her nose. He'd kissed her nose, of all things.

Her skin tingled and a strange warmth stole through her. Okay, so it was nice, but still. It wasn't what she'd expected.

The sound of his footsteps drew her from the emotional push-pull. Her eyes popped open in time to see him disappear outside and she found herself alone.

Her chest hitched at the thought. A ridiculous re-action because the solitude gave her a few minutes to pull herself together and remember that she wasn't here for *nice*.

She drew a deep, shaky breath and reached for a nearby spoon to stir the meat that was slowly starting to brown.

She spent the next few minutes stirring and trying to

convince herself that she hated every second. Even if the meat did turn the most perfect shade of sizzling brown.

"It looks good."

The deep voice stirred the hair on the back of her neck and sent a jolt of awareness through her. Her hands trembled and her grip on the spoon faltered. It fell into the pot and landed with a splat on top of the pile of beef.

Billy's deep chuckle sent a tingle through her body. "I usually add cayenne at this point." He eyed the sinking spoon. "Trying something new?"

"Maybe." She scooted a few feet away toward the utensils drawer. "Do you always sneak up on people?" She tossed him a sideways glance as she rummaged for a pair of tongs.

His eyes twinkled and his sensuous mouth crooked. "Are you always so touchy when you cook?"

"I don't cook very much." The words were out before she could stop them. This wasn't about having a conversation. It was about getting to the good stuff. The physical stuff. "My mom tried to teach me, but I was never very interested. In my mom, not the cooking." The words were out before she could think better of them.

"I pretty much taught myself. Jesse never could cook to save his life, and Cole was always too busy chasing women."

"And that never kept you very busy?"

His grin was slow and wicked and her heart skipped a beat. "I never had to do any chasing, sugar. They come running after me."

Before she could stop herself, she popped him with a

dish towel and his grin faded into a look of pure shock. "What the hell?"

"You're too cocky for your own good," she said, turning back to the pot of meat. She retrieved the spoon with the tongs and set them to the side. "Somebody needs to bring you down a notch or two."

"So why didn't you like being in the kitchen with your mom?"

"I thought we changed this subject."

"You brought it up."

"My mom is the type of woman who bends over backward for any and every man in her life. She bent and they let her. They used her."

"Your dad, too?"

"My dad was the worst. She was with him the longest. She did everything for that man, but it wasn't enough to keep him at home. To keep him faithful. He walked out on us when I was thirteen years old. My mom's been looking for his replacement ever since. The trouble is, she keeps finding him and the pattern repeats all over again."

Her mind rushed back to the past and she saw her mother standing in the kitchen, slaving over her father's favorite red velvet cake. She'd made four batches of cooked white frosting before she'd managed to get it right, and all for nothing. He'd never even come home from work that night. Instead, he'd gone straight to the local beer joint and spent the night with some barmaid.

He'd come home smelling like Emeraude and Aqua Net the next morning and her mother had simply sliced the cake and served him a slice as if he was fresh out of the shower after a hard day's work.

"I'll never kill myself for a man like that." She didn't mean to say the words, but they came out anyway.

"You shouldn't have to."

She turned then and her gaze caught his. Sympathy gleamed so hot and bright in his eyes and a sudden rush of warmth went through her. A feeling that had nothing to do with the lust that burned between them and everything to do with the fact that Billy Chisholm actually understood her feelings. Even more, he was on her side.

Yeah, right.

"So, Eli taught you to cook?"

"Sort of. He taught me to just throw it all together and see what happens. I practiced on my own to come up with this recipe." He grabbed a bottle of garlic and handed it to her. "Add a little bit of this."

She grabbed the spice, popped the cap and shook once, twice, a third time.

"That's not enough," Billy's deep voice whispered into her ear as he came up behind her. One hand slid around her waist while the other closed over hers.

"You don't have to do this." *What the hell?* a voice whispered. This was exactly what he needed to do. To get them off the topic of mothers and brothers, and back onto the real reason she was here—sex.

She knew that. But her heart beat double time anyway, as if there was much more at stake than a little mattress-dancing.

The fingertips that held her frantic grip on the garlic

powder slid down until his thumb massaged the inside of her wrist. The heat from the bubbling chili drifted up, bathing her face and making her cheeks burn. Air lodged in her chest and she couldn't seem to catch her breath.

"Give it another shake," Billy murmured, the words little more than a breathless whisper against the sensitive shell of her ear.

She wanted to say something, to argue the point, but she couldn't seem to find the words.

"That's it." His thumb slid from the inside of her wrist, up her palm, leaving a fiery trail. "Now you're cooking like a real champion."

Boy, was she ever.

She became instantly aware of his hard male body flush against hers, her bottom nestled in the cradle of his thighs. His erection pressed into her, leaving no doubt that he was turned on.

Extremely so.

Her mouth tingled and she had the insane urge to turn into the warm lips nuzzling her ear.

A perfectly natural reaction, given the situation. A perfectly physical reaction.

Yet there was more at stake at the moment.

She felt it in the double tap of her heart. In the strange fluttering in the pit of her stomach. Both physical reactions. The thing was, she'd never felt either with any man before. Cowboy or otherwise.

Because Billy wasn't just any man.

He was *her* man.

The thought struck and before she could drop-kick it out of her mind, she turned.

And then she wasn't just thinking about kissing him, she was actually leaning forward, sliding her arms around his neck and pressing her lips to his.

15

SHE WAS KISSING HIM.

Billy felt a split second of panic as her lips parted. Her tongue touched, swirled and teased. She didn't hold anything back.

Which meant he should have reined in his response right then and there. This wasn't about sex. It was about like. About spending time together and figuring out if she felt even half of what he did.

At the same time, there was something desperate about her touch. As if this kiss was different from all the others they'd shared over the past few days.

The thought intoxicated him even more than the sweet taste of her lips. He planted one hand on the back of her head, tilted her face to the side and kissed her with everything he had.

He nibbled her bottom lip and plunged his tongue deep, exploring, searching. When he couldn't breathe, he slid his lips across her cheek and along her jaw. His mouth slipped to her neck and he pushed her hair to the side, inhaling her sweet scent. She smelled of peaches and warm, feminine skin. He breathed her in for a long, heart-pounding moment and closed his eyes. He thought of all the things he wanted to do with her.

Everything.

He ached to see her soapy and wet in his shower. Naked and panting against his sheets. Smiling and laughing across the breakfast table—

He killed the last thought and concentrated on the lust that rolled through him like a ball of fire that dive-bombed south. He edged her sideways until they were clear of the stove, then bent her back over the counter-top and captured her lips again.

He fed off her mouth for several long moments, tasting and savoring, before nibbling his way down the sexy column of her throat.

His penis throbbed, and it was all he could do to keep from shoving his zipper down, parting her legs and plunging fast and sure and deep inside her hot, tight body.

Now. Right. Friggin'. *Now.*

He wouldn't.

He didn't want just sex anymore. He wanted to know that she felt something more.

Love?

Hell, he was the last person to even know what love was. He'd never been in love. He'd spent his younger years barely surviving, and his teenage years trying to do more than just survive. He'd never had time for more than sex.

He didn't have time for it now.

But he wanted it.

Not that he wanted her to fall madly in love with him or anything crazy like that. He just wanted to know that she at least felt *something* for him.

And that meant slowing down enough to give her time to feel. To think. To want.

He slammed on the brakes and concentrated on the small cry that bubbled from her lips when he licked her pulse beat. He liked pleasing her, so he held tight to his control and paced himself. With each touch of his lips, she sighed or gasped. The sounds fed the desire swirling inside him.

When he reached the neckline of her dress, he traced the edge where her skin met the material with his tongue and relished the breathy moan that slipped past her full lips. His hands came up and he touched her, a featherlight caress of his fingertips over the soft fabric of her dress. He traced the contours of her waist, her rib cage, the undersides of her luscious breasts.

He slid his hands up and over until he felt the bare skin plumping over her neckline. Heat zapped him like a live wire and his pulse jumped. He tugged at the bodice. Buttons popped and her luscious breasts spilled over the top.

Grabbing her sweet round ass, he lifted her, hoisting her onto the countertop. He stepped between her legs and caught one ripe nipple between his lips. He suckled her and she arched against him.

He pushed her back down, still sucking as he caught

the hem of her dress. He shoved the material up until he felt the quivering flesh of her bare thighs.

He didn't mean to touch the softest part of her, but suddenly he couldn't help himself. He slid a finger deep inside her slick folds and her body bucked. He drew away from her swollen nipple and caught her delicious moan with his mouth. He plunged another finger inside, wiggling and teasing.

He wanted to feel every steamy secret. Even more, he wanted to taste her.

Tearing his mouth from hers, he worked his way down, kissing and teasing and tasting until he reached the dress bunched around her waist. He glanced up and his gaze caught hers for a brief moment before he dipped his head.

He licked the very tip of her clit with his tongue and she shuddered. She opened wider, an invitation that he couldn't resist. He trailed his tongue over her clit and down the slit before dipping it inside.

She was warm and sweet and addictive, and suddenly he couldn't help himself. Hunger gripped him hard and fast. He sucked on the swollen nub and plunged his tongue inside until her entire body went stiff.

"Come on, baby," he murmured. He gripped her thighs and held her tight. "Let go."

A few more licks and she did. A cry rumbled from her throat and tremors racked her body. He drank her in, savoring her essence until her body stilled.

Then he pulled away and stared down at her.

"Please. Just do it. Do it now," she murmured, her

eyes closed, her face flushed. Her chest rose and fell to a frantic rhythm that made his groin throb and his entire body ache. She was so beautiful. So damn sweet. He wanted her more than he'd ever wanted any woman.

But even more, he wanted her to want him more than she'd ever wanted any other man.

"I think the chili's burning."

Her eyelids fluttered open. "What?"

He took a huge drink of oxygen and forced his hands away from her. "I need to turn the heat down."

Boy, did he ever.

"Chili? You're worried about the chili?" Her gaze swiveled toward the stove and the stream of smoke that funneled from the gigantic pot. "Oh, no." Her cheeks fired a brighter red as she shoved at the hem of her skirt and tugged up her bodice.

City gal Sabrina Collins blushing, of all things. It was definitely a first. He liked it. He liked it a hell of a lot.

What he didn't like was that she'd scrambled away from him faster than he could blink. As if she'd just realized she'd made a big, big mistake. One that had nothing to do with the smoke that slowly filled the room.

"I've got an early meeting tomorrow," she said as he turned his attention to the stove. "I really should go."

"Duty calls."

"I know I'm supposed to help so we can get busy later, but—what did you just say?"

He winked. "If you have to leave, you have to leave."

"That's okay with you?"

"I'd rather you stay and help me finish this batch, but I know you've got a lot on your plate."

"But our arrangement—"

"—will wait." He arched an eyebrow. "You can wait, can't you?"

"Um, yeah. Sure. I just thought you needed some sleep."

"I'm sure I'll be pretty tuckered out after all this chili. I'll take a rain check tonight."

"Well, all right then." She turned and snatched up her purse. "I'll just head out."

"Sweet dreams," he called after her.

"Yeah, right," she muttered, and a rush of satisfaction went through Billy. He'd won tonight's battle.

Now if he could only win the war.

THEY WEREN'T HAVING SEX.

It had been two days since the chili incident and other than a few hot kisses and some heavy petting, she wasn't any closer to working Billy Chisholm out of her system. She needed the real deal for that.

At least that's what she was telling herself.

She needed him inside her and her wrapped around him and she needed an orgasm. A major, mind-blowing orgasm during the actual deed. The preliminary stuff... It just wasn't the same thing.

At least that's what she was telling herself.

Because no way was she so wound up because she was nervous. Afraid. She had only two days left in Lost Gun before the rodeo finals and no doubt that she would add the last twenty cowboys to her list and meet her goal. Twenty-one counting Billy, who'd promised she could sign him up when all was said and done.

She certainly wasn't so antsy because she didn't want to sign him up. Because she wanted him for herself. For the next two days and beyond.

Real sex.

That was all she needed to relieve the tension in her shoulders and ease the anxiety knotting her stomach. She held tight to the truth as he ended the heavy-duty petting session that had started the minute she'd arrived on his doorstep late Friday night, after a long day at the festival and enough profiles to push her that much closer to her goal.

All the more reason she should have headed to the saloon to celebrate with Livi. They were going to make it, to secure their funding.

But Sabrina wanted more. She hadn't given up on her story, even if all of the research she'd done on Silas Chisholm made her want to wrap Billy in her arms and hug him for all the grief he'd suffered thanks to his father. A story was a story. If she ever wanted to make it as a real journalist—and she did, even if it wasn't half as much fun as she'd anticipated—she had to learn to separate her emotions from the situation. She would. She would never have another opportunity like this one. Billy had seen the fire. He'd been an actual eyewitness to the events that had unfolded that night. He was her inside track on the story of a lifetime. One she desperately needed if she ever wanted to move beyond running a web hook-up service. She needed this story. Even more, she needed sex. And so she'd headed up to Billy's cabin instead.

And straight into his bed.

For about fifteen minutes, she felt convinced her dry spell was about to end. But then he pulled away, kissed her one last time with enough passion to make her hormones cry, and then he rolled over to go to sleep.

Sleep.

Seriously?

She tossed and turned and did everything she could to keep him up, but then he slid an arm around her and pulled her back flush against his body. Her hopes soared one last time, but then she heard the deep snore directly in her ear.

"Really?" she muttered, barely resisting the urge to pinch the hell out of his arm.

But the solid muscle wrapped around her did feel good and she found herself relaxing a little. Enough to stop contemplating revenge plots and actually close her eyes for a few moments. It *had* been a long day and this was sort of nice, too.

Not that she was falling asleep.

SHE FELL ASLEEP.

The truth sank in several hours later when her eyes finally popped open and she realized that it was almost five o'clock in the morning.

She'd fallen hard and fast, but he hadn't.

Her gaze went to the empty stretch of sheets beside

her. Obviously he'd been the one to beat a hasty retreat this time and now she was all by her lonesome.

All the better.

That meant she didn't have to worry about picking herself up and getting the hell out of Dodge before he opened his eyes. He'd beaten her to the punch and now she could close her eyes and go back to sleep for a little while. And she certainly wasn't going to wonder where in the world he'd run off to at five o'clock in the morning. Probably some early-morning training session. Or some interview with PBR executives. Or maybe he was helping out at the Gunner Ranch until Pete and his new wife returned.

Not that she cared.

She rolled onto her right side and punched the pillow a few more times before snuggling back down. There. She was going to close her eyes and she wasn't going to remember the tenderness in his eyes when he'd fed her a taste of chili the night before. Tenderness? Yeah, right. That had all been part of the foreplay, which had been part of the sex.

That's all last night had been.

Even if it had felt like an actual date.

She nixed the thought. A date implied like, and no way did he like her. And she certainly didn't like him.

Her chest tightened and her eyes popped open. She rolled onto her left side, scrunched the pillow under her head and snuggled down. There. Now she was going to close her eyes, and she wasn't going to remember the way he'd pulled her close the minute they'd hit the sheets and held her as if she was the most important thing in his life—

Her eyes popped open again and she rolled onto her back.

She sat up and climbed out of the bed. A few steps and she found herself in the hallway. The hardwood floor was cool beneath her bare feet, but it did nothing to ease the fire burning inside her as she walked toward the kitchen. A glass of ice water would do the trick. Or maybe she could stick her head in the fridge until she started to calm down and think rational thoughts.

Like how excited she was that she was *this* close to meeting her quota and getting the hell out of Lost Gun for good.

At the same time, she still hadn't managed to put together a decent story about the death of Silas Chisholm. Even more, she hadn't managed to find a date for Melba Rose and she was no closer to hooking up Sarah Jean from the bakery and—

Seriously?

She wasn't a matchmaker. She was a journalist biding her time until she got her big break. Melba and Sarah would just have to find their own men because she had ten more cowboys to sign up and a story to write before she left town.

And she *was* leaving.

"Can't sleep?" The deep, husky timbre of his voice met her the minute she reached the doorway to the kitchen.

She found Billy standing at the kitchen counter. The

sight of him wearing nothing but a pair of snug, faded jeans stalled her heart for a long moment. Soft denim molded to his lean hips and strong thighs, and cupped his crotch. A frayed rip in the denim on his right thigh gave her a glimpse of silky blond hair and tanned skin and hard muscle and... *Oh, boy.*

She'd seen him without a shirt before, but she hadn't really *seen* him. She'd always been too anxious to get to the main event to really take a long, leisurely look, and too determined the morning after to ignore him.

He had the hard, well-defined physique of a rough-and-tough bull rider. Broad shoulders. Muscular arms. Gold hair sprinkled his chest from nipple to nipple before narrowing into a thin line that bisected his six-pack abs and disappeared into the waistband of his jeans. Her gaze was riveted on the hard bulge beneath his zipper for several fast, furious heartbeats before shifting north.

"Hungry?" he asked.

She swallowed. "You have no idea."

"Me, too." He held up a forkful of pancakes. The aroma of melted butter and sweet syrup hit her nostrils. Her stomach grumbled and he grinned. "I've got a big stack if you want some." She didn't miss the heat that simmered in the bright violet depths of his eyes, which made her all the more confused as to why he'd stopped before the main event last night.

He obviously wanted her.

She could see it.

Feel it.

But then his gaze darkened and he stiffened, as if he'd just remembered some all-important fact.

"Come on and I'll get you a plate," he offered.

Pancakes, a voice reminded her. *As in breakfast. As in the morning after.*

But it was still dark out and she was too hungry and, besides, they hadn't actually done the deed last night, which completely killed the notion of a morning after.

"They're homemade," he added. Determination gleamed hot and bright in his gaze, along with a glimmer of possessiveness that said he'd just climbed onto a monster bull for the ride of his life, and he had no intention of letting go.

Not now.

Not ever.

And damned if that notion didn't excite her even more than the prospect of hot, breath-stealing sex.

She smiled. "Let's eat."

16

BILLY HAD NEVER been a big believer in luck. Good fortune came through hard work and talent, and when things went wrong, there was usually a damn good reason behind it. Lack of motivation. Fear. Laziness.

He'd learned that from Pete and his older brothers.

A man made his own luck. It never just waltzed in on its own.

But as he watched Sabrina walk into his kitchen, he couldn't help but reevaluate his position. He fully expected her to turn and run, the way she did every morning. Yet here she was, standing right in front of him wearing nothing but his T-shirt and a look that said she was none too happy about it.

Still, she was here.

And damned if Billy didn't feel like the luckiest man on the planet.

He turned back to the stack of pancakes he'd just made. Grabbing a nearby plate, he fed a few golden cakes onto it. "Syrup?"

"Please."

He grabbed the bottle and poured a hefty amount of brown liquid before handing her the cakes. He watched as she cut into the stack and stuffed a bite into her mouth.

Her features softened and pure ecstasy rolled across her face, the sight like a sucker punch to his gut.

"The chili I could see," she murmured around a mouthful, "but pancakes, too?" Her gaze caught and held his and the air rushed back into his lungs. "I'm impressed."

"Glad to hear it."

"Did your older brothers teach you this?"

"Jesse can barely heat up a frozen waffle in the toaster. And Cole's the fast-food king." He shrugged. "Eli was always the cook in the family."

"My partner and best friend Livi did most of the cooking in our dorm room. Mostly microwave stuff, though. That, or we did takeout."

"What about your mom?"

"She could outcook Rachael Ray, which is why I stay as far from the kitchen as possible." She took another bite and he had the distinct feeling she wanted to change the subject.

"So how long have you and Livi been friends?"

"Since freshman year. I didn't know if I was going to like her at first. We were so different." When he arched an eyebrow, she added, "I know I don't look like it, but I was a small-town country girl at one point in time."

"You say that like it's a bad thing."

"It is. It was." She shook her head. "I hated being from a small town. I hated the fact that we had to drive two hours just to get to a mall. I hated everybody being in everybody's business. I hated that everybody knew what a rat bastard my dad was, while my own mom buried her head in the sand."

"Maybe she wasn't as clueless as you think. Maybe it just didn't matter."

"How's that possible?"

"Maybe she accepted him the way he was." He ate another bite of his own pancake. "My dad was a son of a bitch. There's no denying that. He did some really awful things and my older brothers hated him for it." He shrugged. "I didn't."

"But you were young—"

"That had nothing to do with it. I knew what he was, but it didn't matter. He was still my dad." He shrugged. "Maybe your mom knew, too, but she just accepted it because that's the way he was and she loved him anyway."

"Love had nothing to do with it. She was afraid of being alone."

He shrugged. "I can see that. A single mom on her own seems pretty scary to me."

"Being a mom didn't have anything to do with it. She didn't stay for me. She stayed for her own selfish reasons."

"You sure about that? It seems pretty selfless to sacrifice your own happiness to stay in a bad relationship and try to make it work. To give your kid a real family." When she didn't look convinced, he added, "And sometimes it's just easier to run from the truth than stand and face it."

"Profound words from rodeo's biggest good-time cowboy."

He winked. "Just call me Dr. Phil."

A companionable silence engulfed them for the next few minutes as he watched her finish off her pancakes. A glimmer of sadness lit her eyes and he had the crazy urge to haul her into his arms and hug her tight until the look disappeared.

But he knew if he touched her, he wouldn't be able to stop. It had taken every ounce of strength not to finish what he'd started earlier that evening and his control was shaky at best.

"You're lucky she at least tried," he heard himself say, eager for something to distract himself from the sudden image of her naked and panting beneath him. "My dad never gave a lick about anyone other than himself, otherwise he would have straightened up his life and played by the rules. Folks call him a career criminal, but being a criminal isn't a career. It's a death sentence."

"What really happened that night?"

"He robbed a bank, went home, had too much to drink and fell asleep with a lit cigarette. End of story."

"Where were you?"

"Jesse had this part-time job at the training facility. He used to feed the bulls after school, shovel manure— that sort of thing. Jesse didn't want us going home without him, so he kept us at the training facility. When Silas drank, which was most of the time, he wasn't the nicest guy, and Jesse didn't want him beating the crap out of us."

"He doesn't sound like much of a man."

"He wasn't, but he was still our dad."

"It seems to me, Jesse was more like a dad to you."

Her words eased the tight feeling in his chest just a little.

Because she was right. Jesse had been more of a dad than Silas ever would. More of a man. A good man. Honest. Loyal. Trustworthy.

But then Jesse wasn't a carbon copy of their old man.

It's just hair, bro. You're nothing like him.

That's what Jesse had told him too many times to count, whenever Billy stared into a mirror and saw his old man in his reflection, but he'd never let himself really believe it.

Until now.

Until Sabrina Collins looked deep in his eyes and said the very same thing.

There was just something about the conviction in her gaze, the sincerity, the compassion that hit a button deep inside him and made him think that he could be different. That he *was* different.

"I look just like him," he said, because old habits died hard and Billy had been reminding himself of the past far too long to stop now. "That's what everybody says."

"So? I look like my great-aunt Mildred, but I'm nothing like her." When he arched an eyebrow, she added, "She's a lesbian. She just moved in with her bingo partner and adopted a new cat. I'm not a cat person either.

I like dogs. Not that I have time for one, but when I do, I plan on getting a blue heeler."

"Heelers are great. Eli used to have a red heeler pup that always hung out at the training facility. Cole and I used to play with him while we were waiting for Jesse to finish up work. That, or we'd play Lego or Hot Wheels. Then we'd all walk home together."

"Were you together the night of the fire?"

He nodded. "Jesse finished up late and we were a good hour past our usual time. Otherwise, that night was just like any other until we saw the flames. We knew it was our house that was burning even before we got close." His gaze caught and held hers. "We just knew."

Ask him.

Ask him when? Where? What? Why? How?

There were so many unanswered questions and this was the chance she'd been waiting for. Her opportunity to get the inside scoop. There had been dozens of reports on what had happened to Silas Chisholm and the money he'd stolen, but no interviews with the actual witnesses. The Chisholm brothers had answered all the police's questions, but they'd never given an actual one-on-one to the press.

And they never would.

Which made this moment all the more valuable.

Billy was talking freely about that night, opening up to her. All she had to do was ask the really tough questions and she could write an exposé that would lead her to a real journalism career and stir up the past for all three of the Chisholm brothers yet again.

And while Billy didn't seem all that upset to be walking memory lane, she didn't miss the tight lines around his mouth or the sudden tensing of his shoulder muscles, or the fear that flickered deep in the depths of his gaze.

For all his bravado, the past pained him. And damned if she could make herself probe the wound.

"Wow," she blurted, stuffing a forkful of pancake into her mouth and killing her one shot. Surprisingly, that fact didn't bother her nearly as much as it should have. Because she wasn't cut out to be a journalist? She didn't know. She only knew that now wasn't the time to figure it out. She had more important things to worry about. Like Billy. And the hurt she'd glimpsed. "These are really good. You have a recipe?"

"No, but I could teach you." He eyed her. "That is, if you want to learn."

And where she'd avoided the kitchen her entire life because it reminded her of her mother, suddenly whipping up a batch of pancakes with hot, hunky Billy Chisholm didn't seem all that bad. Especially since it chased the fear from his gaze and filled it with a hopeful glimmer.

She smiled. "It's about time I learned how to make something other than ramen noodles."

17

"THIS ISN'T PART of our agreement." Sabrina stood on the front porch of Billy's cabin later that morning and stared at the black-and-white horse he'd just walked from the barn.

He tipped his hat back and the devil danced in his gaze. "How's that?"

"For one thing, it's daytime. Morning, to be exact, and I don't do mornings."

"I'll be busy tonight winning this rodeo, so just think of this as a schedule change."

"I wasn't planning on a schedule change, but suppose I go with it. Our agreement still doesn't state anything about riding horses." Or making pancakes, or laughing and talking until the sun came up about his life growing up on the Gunner spread and her life in Sugar Creek. But they'd done it anyway, and she'd enjoyed every moment. "It's all about sex."

"Trust me," he murmured, the early-morning sun bathing him in a bright light that made him seem even darker and more dangerous, "so is this." Billy winked. "We're riding double."

"So we will be fooling around?"

His grin was a slash of white beneath the brim of his hat. "That's the plan."

"Really? Because it's been four days." The grin widened and she stiffened. "Not that I've been, um, counting."

"Actually, it's been four days, three hours and fifty-two minutes." She arched an eyebrow and his expression went serious. "I've been the one counting."

Her heart did a double thump and the butterflies started to flutter low in her belly. "So, um, how exactly is this going to work?"

"Well, I'll be in back and you'll be in front." He let the words hang between them for a long moment. "Use your imagination, sugar."

"What if I fall off?"

"I've never lost a partner yet."

"Meaning, you've done this before?"

"Ridden a horse? Yes." His gaze darkened for a split second and a serious note touched his expression. "Riding double? No. You'll be the first." The look went from serious to seductive. "But I've thought about it a time or two." His eyes twinkled. "Or three."

"And here I thought you spent your time dreaming about PBR titles."

"I did up until I met you."

His words sent a burst of warmth through her that crumbled her defenses. She glanced down at the oversize T-shirt she wore. The soft cotton hit her below the hips. Beyond that, her legs and feet were bare. "I'll have to get dressed—"

"You're fine just like that." He stared at her as if he could see the slinky undies beneath. "The less you have on, the better."

If the words weren't enough to convince her, the hungry look on his face left no doubt that the next few hours would, indeed, be all about sex.

A shiver worked its way through her, along with something else. A rush of hesitation, because despite his words, this wasn't just sex. The past few hours, even the past few days, had changed things between them. Upped the stakes.

"You're not scared, are you?" Challenge fueled his words and lured her down the steps, when every ounce of sanity told her to climb into her car and get while the getting was good. That, and he was smiling at her. And she had a really, *really* hard time thinking straight when he smiled like that.

"Of you? Hardly."

He threw a blanket over the horse's back. "So prove it."

The words hung between them for a long moment before she gathered her courage and closed the distance between them. She planted both hands on her hips and stared up at him. "So how do I do this?"

He held out a hand. "Just put your foot in the stirrup and I'll pull you up."

She slipped her hand into his. "I hope you have a heavy-duty insurance policy that covers passengers."

"No insurance, but I'd be happy to kiss away any bruises if you get hurt." He hauled her up in front of him and nudged the horse.

They jerked forward and Sabrina grabbed Billy's thighs to keep from teetering to the side.

"Easy." The word whispered through her ear as they trotted forward, and Sabrina clutched him tighter.

"I don't think she heard you," she said over her shoulder.

"I wasn't talking to the horse. I was talking to you." He held the reins with one hand, and moved the other to cover her fingers, which dug into his blue-jean-clad leg. "Relax, sugar." He touched her, his fingers warm and strong and reassuring.

They rounded the cabin and started for the open pasture up ahead. For the next several minutes, Billy kept them moving at a steady walk and Sabrina managed to relax her grip.

"This isn't so bad—*whoaaaaa!*" They pitched forward as he urged the horse to a trot.

Her heart lodged in her throat for the first few moments. But soon, she grew used to the steady pace and her body relaxed. Her grip on his thighs loosened until her hands rested easy on either side and she actually started to enjoy herself.

The wind whipped at her face, catching the edge of her T-shirt and sneaking beneath the soft material to tease her bare skin. She became acutely aware of the powerful thighs that framed hers, his chest a solid wall of muscle and strength behind her.

"Why don't you take the reins." The deep voice in her ears caused her to shiver. Without waiting for a reply, he urged the leather straps into her hands and she found herself steering the horse. "Just remember to keep your grip firm but not tight. And don't jerk. You'll scare her if you do that."

"What if I want to stop?"

"We're not stopping until we're done." She had the sneaking suspicion that he was talking about more than just the ride.

A few frantic heartbeats later, he touched her thigh and she knew she'd been right. His palm burned into her flesh and her grip faltered.

Billy's other hand closed over hers, urging her fingers tight around the leather until he had a proper grip again.

"Focus," he told her.

"You try focusing in a thong."

Laughter rumbled in her ears and danced along her nerve endings in a seductive caress that made her entire body tingle. "I guess that would make it a little difficult."

"More like hot. Is your bottom supposed to burn like this?"

"You have to rise and fall with the horse. Feel the motion with your thighs and let it guide you."

She spent the next few minutes doing her best to tune into the horse. But the only thing she seemed aware of was the way Billy's hands splayed on her bare thighs.

His hardness pressed into her bottom, proof that he'd meant every word he'd said—this was about sex.

If only it felt like sex.

"This isn't right," she murmured out loud before she could stop herself.

"You're trying too hard," he told her. "Just feel the animal and think about something else. Think about me and what I'm doing to you."

"You're not doing anything."

"Not yet."

His fingers made lazy circles on the inside of her thigh and Sabrina's insides tightened. The movement continued for an endless moment before he urged the animal a little faster. The horse picked up the pace even more and so did Billy. His fingers swept higher, his touch more intense as he moved beneath the edge of the T-shirt and higher until he was an inch shy of the moist heat between her legs.

"See," he murmured against her ear, his deep voice gliding over her nerve endings. "You're doing it. You're moving with the horse. Can you feel it?"

The only thing she felt was him. Surrounding her. Filling her senses. Her heart pounded and her nipples tingled and she could barely think, much less form a reply.

"Sabrina? Are you with me?"

Boy, was she ever, she realized when his thumb brushed her clitoris through the thin lace of her thong and sensation speared, hot and jagged, through her body.

She would have dropped the reins if Billy's hand

hadn't been fastened around hers, guiding the horse when all rational thought flew south to the pulsing between her legs.

"You're so wet." His word were more of a groan as he dipped a finger beneath the edge of her undies and touched her slick folds. "So hot and wet and…" His voice faded into the pounding of her heart and the buzz of excitement that filled her ears.

She tilted her head back, resting in the curve of his shoulder as she surrendered herself to the ecstasy beating at her sanity and let him take control, of the horse and her body.

He slid a finger deep inside her and the air bolted from her lungs. He moved with the horse and so did she, shifting just so, riding his fingers the way the two of them rode the animal.

Her body grew tight and hot. The pressure built with each stroke, every thrust, until a cry broke past her lips. Her climax hit her hard and fast, like a zap of lightning that shook her to the bone. Shudders racked her. The blood hummed in her ears.

The horse seemed to slow with her heartbeat, until they moved at a slow, easy walk. Sabrina had never felt as relaxed as she did at that moment with Billy's arms around her, his heart beating at a steady tempo against her back.

The sun blazed high in the sky by the time they topped a small ridge and found themselves overlooking an endless stretch of green grass that gave way to a winding creek.

"It's pretty, isn't it?" he said.

"Very. Is this your favorite spot?"

"It used to be. Actually, this is the first time I've ridden over this way since I've been back. My brothers and I used to come out here to fish."

"Before or after you went to live at the Gunner Ranch?"

"Both. At first, we did it because we had to. But even after Pete took us in, I'd still ride up here every once in a while and throw out a line." His arm slid around her waist and held her. "Jesse hates coming out here because he says it reminds him of all those tough times. But I never really saw it like that. This place reminds me of my brothers and how close we always were." He neared the creek and brought the horse to a stop. "Come on." He slid down and turned to pull her after him.

"What are we doing?" she asked as her feet settled in the lush grass.

"Getting wet." He pulled his own T-shirt up and over his head and walked toward the grassy bank.

She followed. "I think I already beat you to the punch."

His grin was infectious. "Then it's time for me to catch up." He unfastened his jeans and pushed them down in one fell swoop until he stood completely naked. He fished a condom from his pocket and sheathed himself in one deft motion before he turned to her. He grabbed her hand and pulled her close to help lift the T-shirt up and over her head. He pushed her undies down, gliding the lace over her skin until it pooled at her ankles and she stepped free. And then he hauled her into his arms for a kiss that sent a flood of moisture between her already damp thighs.

Sweeping her up into his arms, he waded out into the water and walked toward the small waterfall coming off the cliff above.

A heartbeat later, the cool water rushed over them like a soothing shower, killing the heat of what promised to be another scorching Texas day.

But the relief didn't last long because he pulled her close and then they were kissing again, his hard body pressed to hers, his mouth plundering hers. He moved them deeper into the waterfall, beyond the constant stream of water into the small opening that sat behind the curtain of water.

He urged her legs up on either side of him and lifted her, hoisting her up until his thick erection rested between her slick folds. His large hands cradled her bottom as his mouth shifted to her nipple. His hot tongue flicked the ripe tip and her moan split open the peaceful quiet.

He teased the ripe peak, licking her over and over. Soon his lips closed around her areola and he sucked her so long and deep that she thought she would come apart right then and there. She tilted her head back

He worked her up and down his erection, the friction making her gasp.

With one hand braced on his shoulder, she reached down between them with her other and touched him.

He was hot and heavy and she wanted to feel him inside even more than she wanted her next breath.

"Now. Please."

His grip on her buttocks tightened as he lifted her a few inches, braced himself and thrust deep inside.

Billy ground his teeth against the overwhelming heat that gripped his throbbing erection. Holy hell, she was hot. And tight. And juicy. He closed his eyes and drank in a deep draft of air, determined to gather his control.

But he had none left.

What little he had had been spent that morning, making pancakes and doing his damnedest not to touch her. To take her.

He'd wanted to give her some distance, some space to see if she felt the way he did.

If she actually liked him as much as he liked her.

She did.

He'd seen it in her smile when he'd asked how the website was going. Heard it in her voice when she'd told him about Melba and Sarah Jean, and how she really wanted to help both women find that someone special even though they weren't her usual demographic. Felt it when she'd told him how much she appreciated him sharing his secret pancake recipe.

She liked him and while he wasn't one hundred percent certain she was ready to admit it, she still felt it.

And that was enough.

It had to be enough because his time was running out. The realization had hit him when Eli had called to give him the night's line-up for the finals. Tonight.

Tonight was his chance at a local championship, the first step toward making the finals in Vegas and winning the overall championship to become PBR's best. That's what he really wanted. The one and only thing that had ever really mattered to him. But at the moment, he couldn't think beyond the fact that the rodeo ended tonight, and so did their agreement.

And while he hoped like hell she'd come to realize how she felt about him enough to keep seeing him for a little longer, he wasn't going to miss his one sure shot to be in her arms again.

And now she was here, beneath him, pulsing all around him.

She lifted her hips, urging him deeper and he lost his mind. He backed her up against the slick rock wall of the cave and rode her hard, one arm braced on the wall behind her head, the other holding her close as he plunged deeper, faster, until she grasped his shoulders and moaned again.

A rumble worked its way from deep in his chest as he buried himself fast and sure and deep one final time. He bucked, spilling himself while her insides clenched and unclenched around him.

He gathered her close then, holding her tight as his heart threatened to burst from his chest. The water rushed in the background, masking the frantic in and out of his breath as he fought for oxygen. And his sanity.

A losing battle with her so warm and sweet and close.

Losing? Hell, he'd lost the moment he'd first spotted her at the kickoff dance. He'd lost his head.

And his heart.

The realization hit as he drank in another deep breath and tried to think about the rodeo that night and the bull Eli had said he'd drawn. And damned if he could remember exactly which one it was.

Damned if he cared.

Once he'd calmed down long enough to move, he carried her back under the rushing water and out into the waist-deep river. He walked up onto the riverbank and stretched her out on the soft grass. The sunlight spilled over her, bathing her in a warmth that was palpable. Her eyes were closed, her face flushed. Her lips were pink and swollen from his kisses. Her creamy breasts were tight, the nipples a bright rosy pink. A smooth strip of silky hair bisected the vee between legs that were long and slim, her calves shapely, her feet dainty as they rested on the soft green grass.

He'd pictured her like this so many times, so open and naked and *his*. But nothing he'd cooked up in his imagination had been quite as good as the real thing.

This he could touch, smell, feel.

He reached out and traced one nipple.

Her eyelids fluttered open and she smiled up at him. "I think I like this place."

"Glad to hear it." He leaned over and dropped a kiss on the tip of her nose. "Really glad to hear it."

She smiled and the picture she made burned into his memory and made him think that maybe, just maybe, winning the finals wasn't all it was cracked up to be.

This... *This* was what snagging the top prize felt like.

And where he'd recognized before that he felt something different for her, he hadn't grasped just how different until her lips parted and she smiled at him.

Because this wasn't just like.

This was the real thing.

Blinding, dazzling, mind-blowing *love*.

Not that it changed anything.

Because while he knew she felt something for him, he also knew that it wasn't enough to make her stay. While he'd finally accepted that just because he looked like his old man and had a few of his traits, he wasn't the same rat bastard who'd chosen a life of crime over being a father.

He wasn't his dad.

Any more than Sabrina was her mom.

The trouble was, she didn't realize that and there was no guarantee that she ever would.

She was leaving. He knew it. He felt it when she reached up and touched his face, as if memorizing every contour.

And there wasn't a damn thing he could do about it.

18

"BILLY AIN'T HERE," said the old man as he came around the corner of a bull chute at the rodeo grounds later that morning.

It was almost noon on Saturday after the hottest morning of her life.

And the most jarring.

Something had happened between them. Something big.

Billy Chisholm had lost his precious control, and while a small part of her rejoiced, her brain kept telling her that she was in trouble. Big trouble.

Because a small part of her was rejoicing.

Sabrina ignored the strange warmth zipping up and down her spine and concentrated on the old cowboy standing in front of her. "I'm not looking for Billy." She gave Eli an assessing glance. "I'm looking for you."

"Me? Hells bells, what do you want with me?"

"I want you to fill out a profile for my website."

"You might have hypnotized all the other cowboys

around here with that nonsense, but I ain't fallin' for it. Why, it ain't natural to meet a woman on a computer. Whatever happened to good, old-fashioned courtin'? Meetin' at the Piggly Wiggly and gettin' a whiff of her perfume in the vegetable section? Or watchin' her smile while we share a banana split at the Dairy Freeze? Or holdin' her hand while we head for the church picnic? Why, I ain't had a good mess of potato salad since I don't know when."

"You can still do all of that after you fill out a profile. A profile is the first step to meet someone. Then she emails you and you email her and bam, you hit the picnic grounds. Or the Senior Sweetheart Dance," she added, anxiety racing through her as she glanced at her watch. It was Saturday at noon and she had less than seven hours to find Melba a date. She'd gotten the idea for Eli after paying yet another visit to the senior center and realizing that her choices were severely limited. And then she'd thought of Billy and how much he thought of the old man who'd been like a grandfather to him. And just like that, the idea had popped into her head.

"I ain't messin' with no computer." Eli shook his head. "Can't stand the thing as it is. I told Pete not to go all electronic out at the ranch, but he didn't listen. Now every time there's a lightnin' storm, I can't print out an invoice for a decent order of bull semen. Tried writin' the damned thing, but Pete told me it has to be in the system. System, my ass. It's bull semen, for heaven's sake. Nature's moneymaker. It ain't natural that we're all so damned dependent on technology. Why, if a zombie apocalypse wipes us out, we're all screwed."

"What did you just say?"

"I said we're screwed."

"Before that."

"Dependent on technology?"

"After that."

"Zombie apocalypse?"

"Bingo." While Eli seemed like the last person for Melba, that one statement had zapped a connection between them. Even more, Sabrina had a gut feeling that it would work.

"So forget the computer and just let me set you up on an actual date."

"I can do that?"

"Sure. I can take care of all the details. I've got someone perfect in mind. You can pick her up and take her on a real outing. No pictures or email required."

"Who are we talking about?"

"Her name is Melba Rose and—"

"No." He shook his head. "That woman's got a few screws loose and I ain't going to be the one what gets stuck with her at the dance. Do you know she cried last year when she didn't win queen? Broke down and bawled like a baby. No sirree, not me. I ain't gettin' stuck with no crying woman."

"But I have a good source that tells me she's a shoo-in for queen this year. That means no crying."

"Are you freakin' kiddin' me? The happy cryin' is even worse than the sad cryin'. Women 'round here freak out for everything. That's why I been single all these years."

"Well, if that's the way you want it." She shrugged. "But I hear she makes a mean potato salad."

That seemed to get his attention. "She does?"

"Prize-winning," Sabrina assured him, barely resisting the urge to cross her fingers. She hated to lie, but she was desperate. At the same time, maybe she wasn't lying. Maybe Melba did make a mean potato salad. Sabrina grasped at the hope and went in for the kill. "I heard she even took first place over at the Mason County potato festival."

"Mason County? Whereabouts is that?"

Sabrina wasn't actually sure since she'd just made it up, but desperate times called for desperate measures. She'd said it, and now it was just a matter of going with the flow and following through. "It's up around Dallas or Waco or something like that."

"Mason County, you say?" He seemed to think. "Why, I think I went to a rodeo out there once. They host an annual potato festival, you say?"

"*The* potato festival. The biggest in Texas."

"And Melba walked away with first place for her potato salad?"

"And her hash browns."

"You don't say?"

"Cross my heart." She tamped down on the guilt that swore she was a terrible person for getting an old man's hopes up. But then she'd already gotten Melba's hopes up, too, and she couldn't very well let the woman show up stag to her big night. Besides, all she had to do was pick up a few pints of potato salad at a nearby barbecue joint and Eli would be a happy camper.

Two birds with one stone.

"So are you in?"

"So long as we eat before the dance. Potato salad *and* hash browns."

"They'll be ready and waiting."

The Piggly Wiggly didn't have a deli section which meant that Sabrina had all of four hours to make potato salad and hash browns, and deliver them both to Melba's house before Eli arrived to pick her up at 6:00 p.m.

Worse, she'd never cooked up a batch of potato salad in her life. And the hash browns? A great, big, fat *never.* She had no clue how to do either.

But she knew someone who did.

"Hello?" said a familiar voice after Sabrina hit the call button on her cell phone.

"Mom?"

"Sabrina? Is that you?" Surprise morphed into concern and Sabrina's chest tightened. It had been so long since her last phone call and she could only imagine the horrifying possibilities that would prompt a phone call running through her mother's mind. "Is everything all right?"

"Fine. Sort of. I mean, I do have a problem, but nothing bad."

"What is it? What's wrong?"

"I need to make potato salad."

"Excuse me?"

"And hash browns. And I know you know how to do both, so I thought you might help me out."

"You're cooking?"

"Only because of extenuating circumstances," she blurted, eager to kill the hopeful note in her mother's voice. "I don't really *want* to do it, but I promised someone and I need to follow through." That or she could kiss goodbye any hope that Eli would take Melba to the sweetheart dance.

"Well," her mother's voice carried over the line, "I do have a really good recipe."

But then Sabrina already knew that. Her mother had been the queen of the kitchen, busying herself for hours to avoid the fact that she was waiting for a man who didn't have the courtesy to even call.

Waiting.

Or maybe that had just been her way of dealing with the situation. Of trying to hold on when all she really wanted to do was let go.

The thought struck and try as she might, Sabrina couldn't push it back out. She'd never really talked to her mother about the hows and whys of her relationship with Sabrina's father. She'd never wanted to. It had been easier to point the finger at someone else than to realize that maybe her father had left because neither one of them had been worth staying for. Not her mother.

And not Sabrina.

Of course, she was all grown up now. Enough to know that her father had been the one at fault. But back then she'd wondered. And worried. And so she'd made up her mind to change. To put as much distance between herself and the woman on the other end of the phone so that she could honestly say she was nothing like Arlene Collins. She'd wanted to be different. To be the sort of woman that a man could love.

A man like Billy.

She nixed the thought and focused on the phone in her hand. "Why didn't you leave?" she voiced the one question that had haunted her so many nights as an adult.

"Excuse me?"

"I don't understand. All those years you wasted on a man who didn't return your feelings. Why?"

"I didn't waste those years. I spent them raising you, loving you. Maybe I should have left, but I just kept thinking of what my own mother and father always believed—that a child deserved both parents. Good or bad. At least they were there. I just wanted you to have a complete family."

And there it was. Billy had been right. Her mother hadn't stayed because she'd been weak. Because she'd feared being alone. Rather, she'd feared disappointing Sabrina.

"Your father wasn't perfect," her mother went on. "I knew that when I married him, but he always made so many promises. Boy, the man could talk. Of course, back then I thought it was more than talk. I hoped it was more. And so I gave him a chance. I gave our family a chance."

"At your own expense. You were miserable."

"It wasn't so bad. I had you." She heard the tears in her mother's voice and it made her own eyes burn.

"I'm sorry, Mom. Sorry that you tried so hard only to be disappointed."

"The only disappointment is that you don't get around to seeing me more. I miss you."

The words echoed in Sabrina's ears and filled her with a rush of warmth that pushed away the cold resentment she'd felt for so many years. "I miss you, too, Mom," she murmured.

"Well, now," Arlene sniffled as if desperate to hide a rush of emotion, "About that recipe…"

SABRINA PULLED TO A stop in front of Billy's cabin a half hour later and sent up a silent thank-you that he wasn't there. He had a full afternoon before the finals tonight, from meetings with the rodeo commissioner and the board of directors, to a special TV segment featuring the best of the best, which meant he wouldn't be back until tonight.

Sabrina intended to be long gone by then.

Their time together had ended and while she wasn't quite finished with her business here in Lost Gun—they still had to pick up five final cowboys to meet their quota and Sabrina needed to match up Sarah—she was finished with Billy.

Tonight was the finals. The end of the road.

She ignored the depressing thought and focused on pulling all of the groceries from the backseat. Inside, she headed for the kitchen and started prepping her potatoes.

"You're doing what right now?" Livi asked when Sabrina answered her cell a few minutes later.

"I'm helping out a friend."

"You're hooking up those old women."

"No, I'm not." She was *trying* to hook them up. Big difference. "So where are you?"

"At the saloon. I'm about to pop the top on a bottle of Redneck Rosé."

"Since when do you drink Redneck Rosé?"

"Since it's the closest thing they've got to a bottle of champagne. I got the last handful of profiles."

"No way."

"Way. I spent the morning at the donut shop out near the interstate. You wouldn't believe the number of men who eat donuts at six a.m."

"Cowboys?"

"Every single one of them. That hunky booty call of yours sent them over from the rodeo arena."

"Billy?"

"The one and only. They said he paid them ten bucks each to fill out a profile."

"He what?"

"He paid them and while that violates our strict policy of not soliciting, it doesn't count because we weren't the ones dishing out the cash. So it's all good." Her voice rose an excited octave. "We did it, Sabrina. We're going to get our financing."

"That's great."

So why didn't it feel great?

The question niggled at her for the rest of the afternoon, along with the fact that Billy had paid a handful of cowboys to help her out.

Because he was anxious to send her on her way?

That's what she wanted to think, but she couldn't help but wonder if there was more to it than that.

If maybe, just maybe, he'd done it because he knew how important this was to her.

Because he loved her?

She dismissed the crazy thought.

No way did Billy Chisholm love her. Not that she would recognize the emotion if she saw it coming at her like a freight train. She'd never seen it between her own parents. Never felt it herself.

No, he knew their time together had drawn to a close and he was anxious to send her on her way. Paying off a few cowboys had been the easiest way to do it. Which meant she was going to get a move on, follow the recipes her mother had given her, and get the hell out of his kitchen.

And then in less than twenty-four hours, she was going to leave Lost Gun—and Billy Chisholm—for good.

"HE'S GONE." Billy heard Jesse's voice just outside the closed doorway to the dressing area where he was pulling on his chaps. "You can't talk to him."

"But he promised me an interview."

"About the rodeo," Jesse said. "You want to talk about our dad and that's not happening right now."

"So will you talk to me about Silas?" The familiar voice carried inside and Billy recognized Curt Calhoun, the reporter from the "Where Are They Now?" episode. "You can't expect people to seriously believe that you guys don't know anything about the bank heist. You had to see something? Hear something? What about the money? Surely he mentioned the money? Maybe even slipped a little out of the way before the fire? There was an entire ten hours between the robbery and the fire."

Plenty of time to hightail it out to Big Earl's, give the old man the money, and head back home to celebrate with too much liquor. Which was exactly what Silas had done.

Or so Jesse believed.

But they'd yet to recover the money. Instead, they'd been digging hole after hole, and Billy was starting to think that maybe, just maybe Big Earl and his great-granddaughter were trying to pull a fast one. A ploy to get money out of Jesse and his brothers.

That, or maybe they were after a story of their own.

A way to make a fast buck.

That's what logic told him, but Jesse seemed so damned sure. And while Billy had a hard time putting his faith in Big Earl and Casey, he trusted his oldest brother.

"I'll catch up to him eventually," Curt promised. "You know that. And then I'll ask him all the questions I'm asking you."

"I know, but it won't be tonight. He's got a rodeo to win."

Damn straight he did.

Billy pulled on his shirt and concentrated on snapping the buttons. But with every button, he thought of Sabrina and the way she'd popped off his shirt and slid it down his shoulders and—

Concentrate.

Tonight was all about the ride, not the woman he'd left at home.

Unfortunately, he couldn't help but wonder if she was still there, or if she'd gone back to her motel, or if she was actually sitting in the stands waiting for the bull riding to start.

"Sabrina's here with me," Eli told him when the old man called his cell to wish him good luck.

"And where exactly are you?"

"Picking up Melba. We've got a date for the Sweetheart Dance."

"I thought you were going to be here at the arena?"

"I've taught you everything I know. You're on your own, son. Now if you don't mind, I've got a plate of potato salad calling my name."

"But—"

Click.

So much for Sabrina waiting in the stands, eager for a glimpse of him. She wasn't here, and she wasn't coming, and Billy needed to cowboy up and get on with it.

He *knew* that.

But damned if he could stifle the disappointment that rushed through him as he opened the door and joined Jesse for the short walk to the main arena.

19

LATER THAT NIGHT, after an evening spent spying on Queen Melba and Eli as they twirled around the dance floor at the Sweetheart Dance, Sabrina pulled up in front of the motel to find Billy's pickup parked in her usual spot.

Her gaze swiveled to the man who leaned against her door, arms folded as he waited for her. Her heart jumped into her throat as she drank in the sight of him. He wore a sleeveless white T-shirt with Eight Seconds and Then Some emblazoned in liquid blue. Faded jeans hugged his thighs and calves. Worn brown cowboy boots completed the outfit. His muscular arms were folded, his expression serious as he waited for her. He looked hot and incredible sexy and…worried?

Her pulse quickened and heat uncurled low in her belly as she slid from the driver's seat. Billy pushed away from the door as she started up the walk toward him.

"What are you—"

"You missed the finals," he cut in. His brows knit together and his mouth pulled into a tight line. "You weren't there."

"I didn't see the point. Our business is—" She meant to say *finished,* but he didn't give her the chance.

He pulled her into his arms and hauled her up against his chest. His mouth covered hers. Strong hands pressed the small of her back, holding her close as he kissed her long and slow and deep. He smelled of soap and fresh air and a touch of wildness that teased her nostrils and made her breathe heavier, desperate to draw more of his essence into her lungs.

Excuse me? a voice prodded. *This is a bad idea. A really bad idea. The purpose of missing the finals was to avoid him. Kissing him is hardly an effective avoidance technique.*

She *knew* that, but he was so close and he smelled so good and she'd missed him so much.

"I can't stop thinking about you," he murmured when he finally tore his lips from hers. "I thought about you all afternoon and tonight. And I still won." He seemed surprised by the fact. "I *won*."

"That's really great." She couldn't help the rush of warmth or the smile that tugged at her lips.

"It is," he said, the words more for himself than her. "But it doesn't *feel* great." His gaze collided with hers. "Not half as great as this." He kissed her again, fast and urgent, the way he'd done at the waterfall. "As you," he murmured when he finally pulled away. "I want you so bad."

Want.

That's what his sudden appearance was all about.

He was here for one thing and one thing only. Because his body drove him. It didn't go beyond sex as far as he was concerned. It never would. Even if he did seem different from the smooth-talking charmer who'd approached her that first night.

Honest. Sincere.

There's no such thing for his kind.

That's what she told herself, but she just couldn't make herself believe it. Not with her lips tingling from his kiss and her body buzzing with desire and her heart aching from the fact that she really *had* missed him. Sure, it had only been a few hours, but it felt like more.

Like a lifetime.

Anxiety rushed through her, heightened by the truth that echoed in her head.

This was it.

Her last night in town. Their last night.

And while an encore wasn't part of the agreement, ending things now before she'd had a chance to really say goodbye seemed like the worst idea ever.

She slid her arms around his neck, leaned up on her tiptoes and touched her mouth to his.

The kiss that followed was hot and wild and consuming. Her head started to spin and her heart pounded faster. He tasted of impulse and danger and a touch of desperation that made her chest tighten and her heart ache. As if he needed this as much as she did.

Her hands snaked around his neck and she leaned

into him, relishing the feel of his body pressed flush against hers.

He pulled free long enough to sweep her up into his arms and carry her inside. A few minutes later, they were inside her motel room. He let her feel every inch of his hot, aroused body as he eased her to her feet.

They faced each other then, and she knew he was waiting for her to make the next move, to show him that she wanted this, too.

She unbuttoned her blouse and let it slide from her shoulders. Trembling fingers worked at the catch of her bra and freed her straining breasts. She unbuttoned her skirt and worked it down her legs. Her panties followed, until she was completely naked.

He didn't reach out. He simply looked at her, yet it felt as if his hot hand traveled the length of her body along with his gaze. His violet eyes were dark and deep and smoldering as they touched on every hot spot—her neck, her nipples, the vee between her legs, the tender flesh of her thighs. Desire rushed through her, sharp and demanding, and she reached for him.

She gripped his T-shirt and urged it up and over his head. Her fingers went to the waistband of his jeans. She slid the button free and her knuckles grazed his bare stomach. He drew in a sharp breath, and then another, when she slid the zipper down and her thumb trailed over his hard length.

She hooked her fingers in the waistband of his briefs and tugged his jeans and underwear down with one motion. His massive erection sprang hot and greedy toward her.

She touched him, tracing the bulge of his veins and cupping his testicles. He throbbed at her touch and a surge of feminine power went through her—so opposite the crazy weakness she'd feared for so long.

She relished the feel of him for a few fast, furious heartbeats before he seemed to reach his limit. He drew her near and captured her mouth with his own. He drew the breath from her body with a hungry kiss that made her knees tremble and her hands shake and her head spin. A mix of desperation and desire fueled her response as she met him thrust for thrust, lick for lick, losing herself in the feel of him so close. A moment later, he pressed her back against the bed.

"Don't close your eyes," he murmured. "I want to know how much you like it when I touch you. How much you want me to touch you." He settled beside her and trailed his hand down the side of her neck, the dip at her collarbone, the slope of one breast. "Do you like it when I touch you here?" With his fingertip, he traced the outline of her nipple and watched it tighten in response.

"Yes," she breathed, the word catching on a gasp.

Her nerves came alive as he moved his hand down her abdomen to the strip of hair that bisected her sex. One rasping touch of his callused fingertip against her swollen flesh and she arched up off the bed. She caught her bottom lip and stifled a cry.

With a growl, he spread her wide with his thumb and forefinger and touched and rubbed as he dipped his head to draw on her nipple. Sensation speared her, and she had to fight to keep her eyes open. But she managed. She fixed her gaze on the blond head at her breast and trailed her hands over his shoulders, committing every ripple, every bulge to memory.

Desperate to keep him with her long after she left town.

When he slid a finger deep, deep inside, she moaned. Her fingertips tightened on his shoulders, digging into the hard, muscular flesh.

"You're so wet," he said, leaning back to stare down at her, into her. "So freakin' *wet*."

"So are you." She reached between them and touched the pearl of liquid that beaded on the head of his erection nestled against her thigh. She spread the liquid around the rock-hard shaft and watched his gaze darken.

"If you don't stop touching me, this is going to go a hell of a lot faster than I anticipated."

"I like it fast, and out of control." The words tumbled out of her mouth before she could stop them. "I like *you* out of control."

He shifted and reached for his jeans. His fingers dove into one of the pockets and he pulled out a condom.

Driven by her need for him, she took the latex and tore open the package. She eased the contents over the head of his smooth, pulsing shaft. He pulsed in her hands and hunger gripped her.

She spread her legs and waited as he settled between them. The head of his penis pushed a delicious fraction into her. Pleasure pierced her brain and hummed along every nerve ending. She lifted her legs and hooked them around his waist, opening her body even more. He answered her unspoken invitation with a deep, probing thrust.

Her muscles convulsed around him, clutching him as he gripped her bare bottom and tilted her so that he could slide a fraction deeper, until he filled her completely. He thrummed inside her for a long moment as he seemed to fight for his precious control.

But Sabrina had already lost her own and she wasn't going to go over the edge without him. She lifted her hips, moved her pelvis, and rode him until he growled and gave in to the fierce heat that raged between them. He pumped into her, the pressure and the friction so sweet that it took her breath away.

She met his thrusts in a wild rhythm that urged him faster and deeper and... Yes. *Yes!*

Her lips parted and she screamed at the blinding force of the climax that crashed over her. Billy grasped her buttocks and held her tight as he plunged one last and final time. A groan ripped from his throat as he followed her over the edge.

BILLY COLLAPSED ON top of Sabrina, his face buried in the crook of her neck, her muscles still clenched tightly around him. He felt every quiver of her body, every delicious shudder, every erratic breath. Her heart pounded against the palm of his hand and a wave of possessiveness swept through him. He had the sudden, desperate urge to tighten his hold on her and never let go. Because she was his.

She'd always been his.

Always.

He gathered her close and focused on the steady beat of her heart for several long moments, letting it lull him and ease the exhaustion in his muscles. He was tired. So damned tired. But he'd needed this in the worst way. He'd needed her. He still did.

The seconds ticked by, sleep pulling them both under. But he wasn't ready to give in. Not yet. Not until...

"I love you," he whispered the words that burned inside of him.

Her heart didn't skip a beat as he held her close and he knew she was already asleep. It didn't matter. He had tomorrow to get his point across. Then she would realize they had something special and change her mind about leaving. And all would be right with his world.

If only things were really that simple.

But Billy had been dealt a shitty hand too many times to think that the woman of his dreams would simply throw herself into his arms and life would be set. Instead, he knew good and well that he was in for the fight of his life.

He didn't care.

Sabrina was worth it, and he intended to prove as much. He just hoped she didn't run for the hills before he had the chance.

20

I LOVE YOU.

The words echoed through Sabrina's head throughout Sunday morning, taunting her as she tried to concentrate on entering her last ten profiles. She had to get back on track and forget all about Billy and the fact that he loved her.

Just where did he get off loving her? He wasn't supposed to love her and she wasn't supposed to love him.

No matter how desperate and out of control he'd been at the river, or how he'd taught her to make pancakes, or how he'd held her and listened to her talk about her mother and her father and her past.

Her heart pounded double time and tears burned the backs of her eyes as she tried to concentrate on her computer keyboard and the stats of cowboy one hundred and sixty-one.

James Early Harwell. James liked the occasional glass of whiskey, old Westerns and dancing until dawn down at the local honky-tonk. He was a ranch foreman at a large spread about twenty miles outside of town. The salt-of-the-earth type and every bit as good-looking as Billy Chisholm.

The exact type that her mother had always had a weakness for.

Weak. That's why she'd landed in bed with Billy. Not because he was different or because she sensed there was more beneath the surface. A man who was honest and loyal and all of the things her own father had never been.

Sure, he'd kept his word and handed her a neatly typed profile last night as promised once their deal was done. But that merely proved what she knew deep in her gut—he was a player like all the others, eager to move on to the next conquest.

That, or it means he's a man who does what he says, who keeps his promises.

One of the few she'd ever known. One of a kind. Special—

Stop. Forget him. Forget that he loves you and forget that you love him.

She couldn't. She wouldn't.

She stared at Billy's profile. Her very last one and the ticket to satisfying her investor and launching the website in a major way.

Her fingers went to the keyboard and she mentally commanded them to type. To enter the stats and get it over with. Then it would be really and truly done and Billy would be just another of the masses. Another sweet-talking, sexy-as-all-get-out cowboy with a sweet-as-molasses drawl and enough charm to make even a saint blush. He was perfect for the website. All the more reason to get him entered and get it over with.

Type.

But she couldn't force her fingers to make contact. They wouldn't move and, truthfully, she didn't want them to move.

Because she cared about him. Because she loved him.

Denial rushed through her. No, she didn't love him. She was close...dangerously so. That's why she couldn't make herself enter his stats and throw him to the masses who would be cruising their website in a matter of days, searching for the cowboy of their dreams.

But she wasn't falling all the way, not head over heels, body, heart and soul, in love with Billy Chisholm. Love required trust, and as much as she wanted to, she just couldn't trust a man like him. She wouldn't.

She wouldn't do something so self-destructive as fall in love with a cowboy like Billy Chisholm. She'd come too far, struggled too hard to escape her past to wind up living it once again. Only this time, she would be the one barefoot and pregnant in the kitchen, whipping up the pancakes and waiting for her man to come home.

If only that last image stirred the same distaste that it once had.

"What do you mean you can't see me?" Billy demanded when he stomped into the diner at lunchtime, after a very heated phone conversation. He'd called to ask for a date, no doubt to discuss the bomb he'd dropped the night before. Of course, she'd turned him down.

And turned him down again when he'd called back the second time.

And the third time.

Now here was Billy himself, standing in front of her table, wearing a black T-shirt that read It's All About the Ride and faded jeans and an intense look that made her pulse leap.

"Let me rephrase that—I don't want to see you." There. She'd said it, despite inhaling his all-too-familiar and terribly sexy scent of warm male and leather and him. Her nostrils flared and her lungs filled, and Sabrina damned herself for being so weak.

She wasn't weak. She was holding her own, keeping up her defenses and getting the hell out of Dodge. Fast. Before any more of Melba Rose's friends approached her to find them dates and she found herself agreeing to yet another day in Lost Gun and, more important, before she gave in to the hunger inside her and kissed Billy until her toes curled.

"We need to talk—"

"About last night," she cut in, "I understand completely. You were worked up and so was I and you didn't mean to say what you said."

"Oh, I meant it, all right—"

"Oh, wow, would you look at that? I've got a meeting over at the senior center and I'm late," she screeched, sliding out of the booth and scooting past him as if she'd been zapped by lightning. "Look, you just run along and don't worry that I'm making more out of it than you meant. We all get a little crazed in the heat of the moment. Chemistry is a powerful thing. People mistake lust for love all the time. Just look at the divorce rate. Lust," she rushed on before he could say anything to shake her determination. "Last night was just a bad case of lust, but now it's sated and—"

"Is it?" he cut in, his gaze deep and searching, as if he struggled to see everything she was trying so hard to deny.

"Yes," she declared with as much bravado as she could muster, considering he smelled so good and she had this insane urge to press her head to his chest just to hear if his heart was beating as fast as hers. "It's definitely sated."

He eyed her for a long, breathless moment, and she knew he was going to argue with her. That, or throw her over his shoulder and tote her back to his cabin and make love to her over and over until she developed such a craving for him that she couldn't keep from loving him. And damned if a small part of her didn't want him to do just that. To take the decision out of her hands so that she didn't have to think, to worry, to be afraid of what she felt for him.

What she *almost* felt, she reminded herself. She wasn't there yet. She wasn't in love. Not with him. She *wasn't*.

As if he sensed the turmoil inside her, his fierce expression eased into his usual charming grin that made her that much more wary.

"Listen, I didn't want to tell you this, but I've been writing a story about you and your brothers and your dad. An exposé to launch my journalism career." Okay, so she'd *thought* about writing an exposé, but she hadn't been able to make herself actually do it. Not after hearing the pain in his voice when he'd spoken about his past. Even more, she'd realized she wasn't cut out to be a journalist if it meant stirring up a world of hurt for someone else. She'd always thought that being a big-time journalist would make her happy, but she'd come to realize that just being good at what she did— namely hooking up Melba—had brought her a sense of accomplishment unlike anything she'd ever felt. But Billy didn't know that, and she didn't intend to tell him. "That was the reason I agreed to your proposition. So that I could get close to you and get the real scoop."

He eyed her for a long moment. "So did you?"

"Did I what?"

"Get the scoop?"

"Not exactly, but that's beside the point. The point is I had an ulterior motive. It wasn't just lust. I was using you."

"Where's the story?"

On its way to CNN. That's what she wanted to say, to prove to him that she didn't really care about him. But there was something about the way he looked at her, as if she was *this close* to disappointing him, that blew a hole in her entire facade. She shrugged. "I decided not to write it." So much for pushing him away.

"Because?"

"Because it's over and done with. Silas is dead. The money is gone. Might as well let sleeping dogs lie."

"What if I told you it wasn't? What if I said the money was still out there and there's proof that Silas had a partner?"

She waited for the rush of excitement at the prospect, but the only thing she felt was the desperate urge to kiss him. "Someone else can write about it then."

Something softened in his expression and she damned herself for bringing up the past in the first place. She'd meant to push him away with the news.

If only it didn't feel as if she'd pulled him that much closer.

"Maybe I will write about it," she blurted, gathering up her purse. "Right after I head over to the senior center."

"If you're no longer in lust with me, then I don't have to worry about you jumping my bones while I walk you over."

"I don't need an escort."

"But I do. It's been forever since I've been there, so I thought you could lead the way. I promised Eli I would stop by and let Melba know that he'll pick her up at eight tonight." At her blank look, he added, "Her cell's not working right now and he's tied up at the training facility." He shrugged. "You're going and I'm going. We might as well walk together."

"No." She shook her head. "I can't." She put her purse back down beside her.

"So you're not going?"

"Of course I am. Later. After lunch." She eyed the half-eaten hamburger in front of her. "You just run along and do your business and I'll stop by later. I think that would work much better. I mean, our time together *is* over. Business concluded. You really should get on with your life, and I'm already zooming right ahead with mine."

"You're still here," he pointed out.

She thought of lying. Of telling him she was doing research to blow the roof off him and his family. But she knew he wouldn't buy it any more than she could sell it. She shrugged instead. "I'm only sticking around for one more week, just until I find a decent prospect for Melba's friend. The VFW has bingo on Friday nights. It's also senior-discount night, which means every available man over sixty-five will be there. I should hit pay dirt there if all else fails this week."

"So you're here strictly for Melba Rose?"

"I made a promise."

He eyed her for a long moment. "You're stubborn, you know that?"

"I'm confident, not stubborn. I just know what I want out of life, that's all."

"Let's hope." He winked before turning toward the door. "I'll see you around, sugar."

"Not if I see you first," she murmured to herself as he edged his way around a table and walked out of the diner.

It was all a matter of keeping her distance until she left town. Rationally, she knew that.

It was the irrational urge to run after him and throw herself into his arms that scared the crap out of her, and made her all the more determined *not* to love Billy Chisholm.

SHE LOVED HIM.

With any other woman, Billy might have had his doubts. After all, she'd ditched him last night and given him the brush-off just now. Talk about rejection.

But this was Sabrina.

Bold, sassy, sexy as hell and scared.

Business concluded, she'd said.

He might have believed her, except that he'd seen the wariness in her eyes, heard the desperation in her voice. There'd been none of the cool confidence of a woman completely uninvolved, none of the nonchalance of someone ready to turn her back and walk away because she didn't feel anything for him.

Even more, she was still here.

While he had no doubt that she meant to keep her promise to Melba's friend, he knew that was just an excuse to stick around. Because she wasn't half as sure about leaving as she'd been the night they'd met.

Yep, she loved him, all right, and so Billy had backed off when he'd wanted nothing more than to pull her close and never let go. He didn't want her to feel pressured or anxious or afraid.

He wanted her willing, sure, certain beyond a doubt. That meant she had to come to terms with her feelings in her own time, and so he decided then and there that he wasn't going to press or push.

Not too much, that is.

He certainly wasn't going to hide away and bide his time and simply hope that she came to her senses. Billy had never been a patient man when it came to something he wanted, and he really wanted Sabrina Collins.

And she wanted him back.

Now and forever.

She just needed a little help admitting it.

21

"THERE'S A WORD FOR THIS, you know," Sabrina said nearly a week after Billy's declaration, when she opened her motel room door to find him standing on her doorstep. Again.

The devil danced in his eyes as he grinned. "Dating?"

She ignored the thumping of her heart and glared. "Harassment. You've shown up every night this week." Every night at exactly the same time. So punctual she could have set her clock by him.

As if his presence, so tall and sexy and reliable, wasn't bad enough, he'd come bearing gifts. Monday he'd shown up with a dozen pink roses. Tuesday, he'd brought a box of chocolate-covered strawberries. Wednesday had been cupcakes from Sarah's bakery. Today?

She eyed the starched Wranglers and pressed Western shirt. He'd traded the frayed straw cowboy hat for a sleek black one, his boots shiny and polished. He handed her a clear florist's box with a wrist corsage nestled inside.

"What's this for?"

"The Elks are having their monthly dinner and dance. While most of the guys are married, there are a dozen or so who are widowers. They gather in the back once the band kicks up to play dominoes and shoot the shit." He shrugged. "I thought you might find a few prospects for Ethel."

"That's a great tip. I'll head over later on—"

"You can't get in without a ticket."

"I'll buy one."

"It's members only. Eli's taking Melba to a movie to-night, so he slipped me his." He waved the slips of paper. "If you want to go, you have to go with me."

"You could be a nice guy and give me one of your tickets."

"And sit home all by my lonesome while you have all the fun?" He shook his head. "Not happening."

She thought of her plans for that night—sitting in her usual booth at the diner, hoping and praying for a new face to come in for the dinner special. She'd met all of two single senior men over the past few days, and both had been spoken for. They'd been picking up dinner for their intended, which meant she needed a new plan.

"Okay, but this isn't a date. That means no funny business."

He arched an eyebrow, his sensual mouth hinting at a grin. "Define what you mean by funny?"

"I mean it, Billy. No funny business. No thinking about any funny business." He didn't look convinced, so she added, "You stay on your side of the truck and I stay on mine. Tonight we're just two friends accompanying one another to a dinner dance."

His grin widened. "Whatever you say."

"Promise me." Her heart pounded for several long seconds as she held his gaze. "Please," she finally added.

As if he sensed her desperation, his expression faded and he nodded. "Just friends."

"THIS IS MY FRIEND, Sabrina Collins." Billy introduced Sabrina for the umpteenth time to one of the elderly couples standing near the punch table and she did her best not to frown.

They *were* just friends, she reminded herself.

Which meant it shouldn't bother her when he said the word. Or left her sitting alone to dance with Mrs. Meyers, the chairperson for the event. Or Mrs. Davenport, wife of the head Elk. Or Mrs. Carlisle, newly widowed and president of the senior ladies' crochet circle.

She watched Billy lead the small, round woman around the dance floor. Her silver hair piled high on top of her head in a monstrous beehive. Bright orange lipstick matched the blinding shades of her flower print dress and her white patent leather shoes gleamed in the dim lighting. With every turn, Sabrina glimpsed the top edge of her knee-high panty hose just below her hemline. On top of that, the woman was three times his age.

It's not like Sabrina had anything to be jealous of if they had been more than friends.

Which they weren't.

"Where's the domino group?" she asked the minute

he walked back to their table. "The band's playing so they should be out back by now, right?" She pushed to her feet. "Lead the way."

"I promised Miss Earline I'd dance with her first."

"Then point me in the right direction and then go dance with Miss Earline."

He eyed her for a long moment and a light twinkled in the depths of his eyes. "If I didn't know better, I'd say you're jealous. But then that would mean that you actually do care and you've made it clear that you don't."

"I'm not jealous, I'm anxious. I've got a lot of work waiting for me back in L.A. I need to get this done and get out of here."

He eyed her for a long moment before he seemed to come to some conclusion. "Follow me."

A few minutes later, she found herself smack-dab in the middle of man heaven. Senior man heaven, that is. There were two dozen widowers in Lost Gun. All eager to find the next Mrs. Right. Provided she could cook as good as Shirley, or clean as well as Bernice, or rub a pair of feet as well as Corrine—God rest her soul. Every single man gathered in the domino room wanted to find a woman, and while a few of them weren't too jazzed about that woman being Ethel, more than half were willing to give her a try.

Two hours later, Sabrina stood on the doorstep of her motel room, profiles in hand, and stared at the man who'd walked her to her room.

"Thanks for tonight." She stuck out her hand to shake his, desperate to keep the distance between them and end the evening before she surrendered to the waves of emotion inside her and plant one on his lips. "I wouldn't have even known about the dinner dance if it wasn't for you and I want you to know that I really appreciate everything."

He stared at her, into her. "I don't want your thanks."

Her hand fell away. "Please, Billy. Don't—"

"I want you."

"It could never work. You live here and I don't. I could never be happy in a place like this." Even if she had grown sort of fond of all the senior ladies that she'd met, and the strong black coffee they served up at the diner and even the chicken fried steak. "I don't belong here."

And then she turned and walked away from him, because after years of clinging to her newfound city ways and keeping her distance from the small-town girl she'd once been, she didn't know if she had the strength or the courage to let go.

Not that she wanted to. She was happy just the way she was.

Wasn't she?

SHE WAS HAPPY.

That's what she told herself the next day as she narrowed down her newfound prospects to the three most perfect matches for Ethel and tried to forget Billy and the way he'd made love to her so furiously at the river. The way he'd tried his best to woo her the past few days. The way he'd stayed close to her at the dinner, his hand at the small of her back, possessive yet comforting at the same time. The way he'd said "I want you" last night.

Distance, she told herself. Out of sight, out of mind.

Which was why she did her best to look the other way when he showed up at the Bingo Hall on Friday night.

With a date.

She eyed the plain young woman wearing a pair of jeans and a Western shirt. She wasn't at all what Sabrina would have pictured, but then she never would have expected him to show up with another woman in the first place.

Proof that she was just as poor a judge of character as her mother. As weak. As gullible.

Really? You told him there was no chance and now you want to throw a pity party because he finally got the message and is now getting on with his life?

She watched him steer the young woman to a nearby table and pure longing shot through her.

Because she wanted to be that woman.

She wanted Billy beside her, smiling at her, loving her.

And he wanted someone else.

Walk away. That's what she should have done. What she'd wanted her own mother to do. But the woman had never had the strength. The balls.

But it wasn't about that, she realized as she stood there, her heart pounding in her chest. Billy had been right. Her mother hadn't stayed because she'd been weak. She'd stayed because she'd been too strong to walk away, to give up her chance at happiness. She'd wanted to fight for it.

Just as Sabrina wanted to fight right now.

And while it hadn't worked out for her mother any

more than it might work out for her, she knew that she would never forgive herself if she didn't at least try.

Panic bolted through her and she was on her feet before she could stop herself. She crossed the room in a few heartbeats and grabbed his arm.

"You can't do this," she blurted as her gaze collided with his. "Please. You can't. Not yet." She paused to drink in a frantic breath. "Not until you hear what I have to say. I love you," she rushed on before she lost her courage. "I always have, I just didn't want to tell you because I was afraid that it would put me at a disadvantage because I've always seen love as a weak emotion. But it's not. It takes courage to love. To admit love. To be in love. My mother had that courage, but my father was the one who didn't. He was the weak one. That's why he left. I know that now. I also know you're not him. You could never be him. That's why you can't do this."

"I have to."

The words tightened a vise around her heart and tears burned her eyes. "You can't. You can't date someone else, because I want to date you. I want to marry you."

He arched an eyebrow at her. "Is that a proposal?"

"Yes. So don't do this. Don't give up on me and start dating someone else."

"He's not on a date." The woman sitting nearby gave her a horrified look. "Hells bells, I wouldn't date the likes of Billy Chisholm. He's just dropping me off on account of my granddaddy's here and he can't see well enough to read his own bingo cards."

"I was doing some work out at her granddaddy's place and she needed a ride. Since you mentioned that you were coming tonight, I figured I would show up, too."

Her gaze swiveled back to Billy as realization hit. "You mean I rushed over here and made a fool of myself for nothing?"

"You rushed over here and made a fool of yourself because you love me and I love you. I do, you know. I have since the first moment I saw you standing at that bar." His grin faded and a serious light gleamed in his eyes. She saw the sincerity in his gaze, and felt it in her heart, and she knew. She gave in to the longing inside and threw herself into his embrace. Strong arms wrapped around her and held her tight.

"I love you so much," he murmured into her hair. "I love everything about you. I love the clothes you wear and the way you look curled up in my bed and the way your eyes glitter when you're mad. Everything. And that's never going to change. No matter how much you try to piss me off or push me away."

She pulled back and stared up at him, tears streaming down her face, happiness overflowing her heart. "You're stubborn, you know that?"

He grinned. "I learned from the best."

Warmth coursed through her and she smiled. "You really think I'm the best?"

"Most of the time. The rest of the time, I think I want to kill you, but I still love you regardless." A serious light touched his gaze. "I meant what I said. I want you. I want marriage and babies and a future, and I want it all with you. Only you. I don't care where we live. If you hate it here, we can move."

"I can't do that."

He stiffened. "Are you saying that you don't want to marry me?"

"I'm saying that I can't move away from here. I actually like it here."

"What about the website?"

"FindMeACowboy.com is Livi's brainchild, and now she's got the funding to make it a reality. I wrote the business proposal and worded all of the profile requirements, but now my work is done. Kat's doing the website and we're well past the idea phase. They don't need me anymore. Besides, I've got an idea of my own I'd like to work on."

"A job at the newspaper?"

"I was thinking more along the lines of a matchmaking service for seniors right here in Lost Gun. I could start with a storefront and then branch out on the web."

"So you're staying?"

"Only if you make an honest woman of me."

He grinned and drew her close. "You've got yourself a deal."

Epilogue

"THIS IS A WASTE of time," Billy Chisholm announced to his two brothers as he tossed a shovel full of dirt to the side and stared at the pastureland rutted with holes in all directions. "We've been digging for over four weeks now and we haven't found anything."

"It's here," Jesse said, but he didn't sound nearly as confident as he once had. "It has to be."

"Unless Big Earl is wrong," Cole pointed out. "The man's ancient. Maybe he hallucinated the connection to Silas."

Jesse shook his head. "Casey confirmed his confession."

"Yeah, but she's got nothing to go on except his word. That brings me back to my first theory—Big Earl could be wrong."

He *was* wrong.

That was the conclusion that Billy had come to weeks ago. Big Earl was wrong and this was just a waste and it was high time the Chisholm brothers admitted defeat and went back to their lives.

A pretty great life, at least in Billy's opinion.

He had one now thanks to the woman waiting back at his cabin. Sabrina had moved in just over a week ago after giving up her apartment in L.A. and moving to Lost Gun for good. They'd announced their engagement just a few days ago and were now planning a wedding to follow on the heels of the PBR finals in November.

Billy hadn't wanted to wait, but Sabrina had been determined to keep him focused on his first championship. Thanks to the Lost Gun win, and the Houston Live Stock Show and Rodeo win right on its heels, Billy was a leading contender. He still had a long way to go, but if he kept performing the way he'd been, he was a shoo-in for the buckle.

"You're going to win," Sabrina had told him. "And then we'll get married. I don't want you worried about anything."

But he wasn't worried. For the first time in his life, Billy felt relaxed and confident and anxious. He wanted to say "I do" even more than he wanted a PBR championship.

But he also wanted to make Sabrina happy and so he'd agreed to wait. But only if she promised to let him help her with the wedding details. Because when it came to Sabrina, he had no problem making up his mind. She was his world. His future.

Which was why he was more than ready to give up this wild goose chase and get home. He'd come clean to Sabrina about the possibility that the money still existed and she'd been nothing but encouraging. There'd been no probing questions, no pushing for information, nothing to indicate that she was a journalist at heart. Because she wasn't. She'd found happiness in her matchmaking business, just as he'd found happiness in his bull-riding.

Still, she'd urged him to look, to help his brothers and lay the past to rest.

At the same time, Billy had already done that. He'd made peace and it was time to let sleeping dogs lie.

"The money's not here," Billy said again. Still, he rammed his shovel into the ground anyway, hard, eager to scoop up as much loose dirt as possible and prove a point.

And that's when he felt it.

The budge of resistance as the hard metal edge met something a few inches below the surface. He signaled Jesse and Cole and the three of them went to work on the spot.

A few breathless moments later, Billy retrieved a nearby lantern and held it up to reveal a large metal box.

His heart pounded in his chest as he broke the lock and pushed open the lid, and then the truth crystallized.

They'd done it. They'd really and truly done it.

After all these years and a world of heartache, they'd finally found the missing money.

* * * * *

Be sure to look for Kimberly Raye's last book in her
trilogy about the sexy Chisholm brothers—
TEXAS OUTLAWS: COLE!
Available from Harlequin Blaze in March 2014.

COMING NEXT MONTH FROM

Available February 18, 2014

#787 CAPTIVATE ME
Unrated!
by Kira Sinclair
What is it about Mardi Gras that makes everyone lose their mind? When Alyssa Vaughn notices a masked stranger watching her undress through her bedroom window, the Bacchus attitude takes over. But wait until she finds out who he is!

#788 TEXAS OUTLAWS: COLE
The Texas Outlaws
by Kimberly Raye
Cole Chisholm's love life is even wilder than the horses he rides. When Nikki Barbie asks him to pretend to be her boyfriend, he agrees...but only if some wild, wicked nights are included!

#789 ALONE WITH YOU
Made in Montana
by Debbi Rawlins
Alexis Worthington is smart, ambitious and has a wild streak that alienated her from her family. Now's her chance to prove herself to them. But working with rodeo rider Will Tanner—she's finding it difficult to behave!

#790 UNEXPECTED TEMPTATION
The Berringers
by Samantha Hunter
Luke Berringer thinks he's finally put his past to rest when he catches the woman who ruined his life—but in Vanessa Grant has he actually found the woman who will heal his heart?

REQUEST YOUR FREE BOOKS!
2 FREE NOVELS PLUS 2 FREE GIFTS!

HARLEQUIN Blaze®

red-hot reads!

YES! Please send me 2 FREE Harlequin® Blaze™ novels and my 2 FREE gifts (gifts are worth about $10). After receiving them, if I don't wish to receive any more books, I can return the shipping statement marked "cancel." If I don't cancel, I will receive 4 brand-new novels every month and be billed just $4.74 per book in the U.S. or $4.96 per book in Canada. That's a savings of at least 14% off the cover price. It's quite a bargain. Shipping and handling is just 50¢ per book in the U.S. and 75¢ per book in Canada.* I understand that accepting the 2 free books and gifts places me under no obligation to buy anything. I can always return a shipment and cancel at any time. Even if I never buy another book, the two free books and gifts are mine to keep forever.

150/350 HDN F4WC

Name _____
(PLEASE PRINT)

Address _____
Apt. #

City _____ State/Prov. _____ Zip/Postal Code _____

Signature (if under 18, a parent or guardian must sign) _____

Mail to the Harlequin® Reader Service:
IN U.S.A.: P.O. Box 1867, Buffalo, NY 14240-1867
IN CANADA: P.O. Box 609, Fort Erie, Ontario L2A 5X3

Want to try two free books from another line?
Call 1-800-873-8635 or visit www.ReaderService.com.

* Terms and prices subject to change without notice. Prices do not include applicable taxes. Sales tax applicable in N.Y. Canadian residents will be charged applicable taxes. Offer not valid in Quebec. This offer is limited to one order per household. Not valid for current subscribers to Harlequin Blaze books. All orders subject to credit approval. Credit or debit balances in a customer's account(s) may be offset by any other outstanding balance owed by or to the customer. Please allow 4 to 6 weeks for delivery. Offer available while quantities last.

Your Privacy—The Harlequin® Reader Service is committed to protecting your privacy. Our Privacy Policy is available online at www.ReaderService.com or upon request from the Harlequin Reader Service.

We make a portion of our mailing list available to reputable third parties that offer products we believe may interest you. If you prefer that we not exchange your name with third parties, or if you wish to clarify or modify your communication preferences, please visit us at www.ReaderService.com/consumerschoice or write to us at Harlequin Reader Service Preference Service, P.O. Box 9062, Buffalo, NY 14269. Include your complete name and address.

HB13R2

Captivate Me

Amid the revelry of Mardi Gras, Beckett Kayne just wanted a
moment of peace. He was enjoying the solitude when a light
snapped on in the apartment across the alley.

She stood, framed by the window. A soft radiance lit her
from behind, painting her in an ethereal splash of color that
made her seem dreamy and tragic and somehow unreal.

Maybe that was why he kept watching. Logically, he realized he was intruding, but there was something about her....

Her eyelids slid closed and her head tipped back. Exhaustion was stamped into every line of her body, but that didn't
detract from her allure. In fact, it made Beckett want to reach
out and hold her. To take her weight and the exhaustion on
himself.

Her hands drifted slowly up her body, settling at the top
button of her blouse. With sure fingers, she popped it open.
And another. And another. The edge of her red-hot bra came
into view revealing an enticing swell of skin.

Tension snapped through Beckett's body. The hedonistic pressure of the night must have gotten to him, after all. Because, even as his brain was screaming at him to give her privacy, he couldn't do it.

It had been a very long time since any woman had pulled this kind of immediate physical reaction from him.

Perhaps it was the air of innocence not even the windowpane and ten feet of alley could camouflage. She was simply herself—unconsciously sensual.

Shifting, Beckett dropped his foot and settled his waist against the edge of the balcony railing. He wanted to be the one uncovering her soft skin. Running his fingers over her body. Hearing the hitch of her breath when he discovered a sensitive spot.

Maybe it was his movement that caught her attention. Suddenly her head snapped sideways and she looked straight into his eyes.

Her fingers stilled. Surprise, embarrassment and anger flitted across her face before finally settling into something darker and a hell of a lot more sinful.

Her arms stretched wide. She undulated, rolling her hips and ribs and spine in a way that begged him to touch.

And then the blinds snapped down between them.

Pick up CAPTIVATE ME by Kira Sinclair, available in March 2014 wherever you buy Harlequin® Blaze® books.

Rules are made to be broken!

Alexis Worthington is smart, ambitious and has a wild streak that alienated her from her family. Now's her chance to prove herself to them. But working with rodeo rider Will Tanner—she's finding it difficult to behave!

Don't miss

Alone with You

by reader-favorite author

Debbi Rawlins

AVAILABLE FEBRUARY 18, 2014,
wherever you buy Harlequin Blaze books.

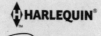